W9-BGZ-011

James Pattinson is a full-time author who, despite having travelled throughout the world, still lives in the remote village where he grew up. He has written magazine articles, short stories and radio features as well as numerous novels.

THE ANGRY ISLAND

When Guy Radford goes to visit an old college friend on the West Indian island of St Marien, he is blissfully unaware of the trouble he is flying into. Divisions of race and wealth have created such tensions between desperate workers and powerful plantation owners that a violent show-down is inevitable. When Radford unwittingly becomes caught in the cross-fire, he finds his own life in danger. And, as the conflict intensifies, the fact that he has fallen in love adds merely one more complication to an already tricky situation . . .

JAMES PATTINSON

THE
ANGRY ISLAND

Complete and Unabridged

ULVERSCROFT
Leicester

First published in Great Britain in 2002 by
Robert Hale Limited
London

First Large Print Edition
published 2003
by arrangement with
Robert Hale Limited
London

British Library CIP Data

Pattinson, James
  The angry island.—Large print ed.—
  Ulverscroft large print series: adventure & suspense
  1. Social conflict—West Indies—Fiction
  2. Adventure stories 3. Large type books
  I. Title
  823.9'14 [F]

  ISBN 0–7089–4954–1

Published by
F. A. Thorpe (Publishing)
Anstey, Leicestershire

Set by Words & Graphics Ltd.
Anstey, Leicestershire
Printed and bound in Great Britain by
T. J. International Ltd., Padstow, Cornwall

This book is printed on acid-free paper

1

No Business

The airfield was a rectangular peninsula jutting out into the bright blue waters of the bay. From the circling airliner it appeared no bigger than a pocket handkerchief. Looking down Guy Radford could see the jumble of buildings that was Portneuf and away in the background a range of mountains.

'So we arrive at the West Indian island of St Marien,' said the man on Radford's left. 'Area approximately three thousand square kilometres and population five hundred thousand. Chief exports: sugar, coffee, tobacco and bauxite. Was formerly a French colony, but gained its independence in 1810 under the revolutionary leader and national hero Albert La Fontaine.'

Radford smiled. 'You seem to be very well informed, Monsieur Blond.'

Monsieur Blond lifted his plump shoulders and let them fall again. He emitted a faintly hissing breath from pursed lips. 'For a salesman it is necessary to know such details.

1

One must understand one's customers. Do you not agree?'

'I'm not a salesman,' Radford said, 'but I have no doubt you're right.'

He was a little tired of Blond. He had had the Frenchman's company from Lisbon and had found it rather overpowering. Blond, a short, stout and somewhat breathless man, had a passion for imparting information, largely worthless. It would come welling up, apparently from some depository in the region of his stomach, to issue from his pale, moist lips like an effusion of gas from a marsh.

And Monsieur Blond's eyes — wide, blue, innocent as a child's — would peer out from an overhang of brows so devoid of hair as to be positively naked. His head was large, and though it could not with any accuracy have been described as bald, it seemed to have been equipped with the absolute minimum of lank brown hair necessary to cover as thinly as possible so wide an expanse of scalp.

The strong scent that flowed from his person might perhaps have emanated from the cream that glued this covering of hair to the skull or it might have been some brand of body deodorant. Whatever it was, it was sweet and sickly, and to Radford's way of thinking, decidedly repellent. He considered himself singularly unfortunate to have been stuck with this particular flight companion and was glad that the journey was almost at an end.

'Although I have done a considerable amount of travelling by air in the course of my work,' Blond said, 'I must confess that I have never quite got rid of a sense of uneasiness when the plane is about to land. Perhaps my imagination is too vivid.'

'There is very little danger surely.'

Blond glanced down at the seat-belt fastened about his ample waist. 'Yet there must be some. Otherwise, why these belts?'

'Just a precaution.'

'As you say, a precaution. You brush the matter aside very lightly. Well, you are young. You have no fears. Once I was like that. Now — ' He gave a self deprecatory smile. He was perhaps fifty years old. Radford was twenty-nine. From Blond's point of view the difference could have seemed large.

The airliner lost height; it straightened for the run in. Blond fell silent. Radford glanced at him and saw that his lips were pressed tightly together and that his hands were clenched.

So he really was nervous.

The ground came up to meet them. There was a slight bump and then they were rolling smoothly down the runway. They came to a stop. Hot sunlight poured in through the windows.

Monsieur Blond gave a sigh and unfastened his seatbelt.

'You see,' Radford said. 'There was nothing to it.'

'When all goes well there never is. When something goes wrong, then it is a different story. Do you stay in Portneuf?'

'No. I shall be staying with friends. They have an estate some way out of town. I expect someone will meet me.'

'You are fortunate. You come for relaxation, I for business. That is how it goes. Some day perhaps we meet again. It has been pleasant to know you.'

'And you, monsieur.'

       ★   ★   ★

Outside, the airport buildings shimmered in the sun. The lightest of sea breezes drifting in over the bay tempered the heat scarcely at all. Radford's shirt was sticking to his back before he had got through the customs.

A Negro in khaki drill slacks examined his passport. The Negro had a gold-braided peaked cap and gold-braided epaulettes. He spoke in French with what Radford took to be a West Indian accent. Radford himself spoke French well, but he found this just a little difficult to follow.

'The purpose of your stay, m'sieu'?'

'Pleasure.'

'No business?'

'No business.'

The passport was handed back. 'I wish you a happy time in St Marien.'

'I am sure it will be very happy indeed.'

★   ★   ★

There were a lot of cars outside the airport building. He could not see Charles.

A taxi slid to a halt in front of him. It was painted a glaring yellow. The driver leaned out, white teeth flashing in the black face.

'M'sieu'?'

He shook his head. Charles had said he would be there to meet him. Yet he certainly was not there. Perhaps he had mistaken the time of arrival. Perhaps he had been unavoidably delayed.

Radford decided it might be a good idea to telephone the Lamartine house and make sure. He had the number. He looked for a telephone booth, but there was not one in sight.

'Does M'sieu' wish for a hotel?' the taxi-driver inquired. 'I can take m'sieu' to the best.'

Again Radford shook his head. The porter who had carried out his luggage was waiting patiently. He was a tall, bony man with arms that seemed to have been stretched by much carrying. The hands reached almost to his knees.

He saw her walking towards him, was astonished to hear her say: 'Guy Radford?'

She was, he would have said, not much over twenty, possibly a year or two. Her hair was pure gold in the sunlight and she was wearing a cotton dress that followed the outline of her figure. It looked worth following.

'Yes, I'm Guy Radford.'

She smiled. He noted that her eyes were grey and that the smile seemed to be in them too. Every part of her that was visible had a smooth, rich sun-tan.

'I'm Antoinette Lamartine. Charles couldn't come, so he sent me instead.' She spoke a purer French than the immigration official or the taxi-driver. Radford found it easier to follow. He wondered whether she had been educated in France. 'Should we go to the car?'

It was an open Ferrari two-seater, bright

red and very sporty. The porter stowed the luggage.

'How did you pick me out?' Radford asked.

'It was easy. Charles told me to look for the most handsome man. It had to be you.'

She got into the car and he lowered himself into the seat beside her.

'Now you're laughing at me.'

'Am I?' She let in the clutch and the car gathered speed down the hot concrete road that led from the airport to the town. 'Anyway, you were the only tall man with fair hair that I could see. Are you sorry?'

'Sorry for what?'

'That Charles didn't meet you.'

'Why should I be sorry when he sends such an attractive substitute?'

She laughed. 'I thought only Frenchmen were supposed to make compliments like that on such brief acquaintance. Englishmen should be cold and unapproachable.'

'It's a legend. You mustn't believe all legends.'

The car moved into the streets of Portneuf. There was a jam of traffic and the pavements were thronged with pedestrians of every shade from white to black. The girl drove skilfully, in absolute control of the red Ferrari.

Radford had forgotten that Charles had a

sister. Presumably Charles had mentioned the fact when they had been friends at Oxford, but that was some years ago and it had passed out of his mind. Antoinette was certainly not much like her brother; Charles was dark. Now and then, however, Radford caught a faint resemblance.

'You had better call me Toni,' she said. 'Everybody does.'

Portneuf had never been planned; it had grown from the roots of the settlement that had sprung up where the River Varne, flowing down from the Blue Mountains, poured itself into the Bay of Hope. From small beginnings Portneuf had spread like a blot of ink until it covered an area of nearly five square kilometres and handled some ninety per cent of the island's export and import trade.

Interesting as the town was, at the moment Radford was rather more interested in his companion.

'I can't remember Charles ever telling me about you.'

'Perhaps he didn't consider I was important enough to mention.'

In profile he could see the almost straight line of her nose and the curve of lips and chin. She had swept her hair back with a movement of the hand and her ear was partly visible, small and delicate, like a sea-shell uncovered by the receding tide.

'I am glad you were able to come,' she said. 'One gets a little bored.'

'It was too great a temptation to resist. Especially since I had just finished with Renfrew and Logan.'

'Who are they?'

'The firm I worked for in Malaya. Mining engineers.'

'Why did you leave them?'

'Wanted a change. I've never liked getting into a groove.'

'I suppose Charles knew that?'

'About my leaving Renfrew's? Yes, I told him in one of my rare letters. He immediately invited me out here.'

'And you accepted.'

'What could be better than a West Indian holiday?'

'It could be more than a holiday.'

'More?'

'Charles has mining interests, you know. You're a mining engineer.'

'You think he might offer me a job?'

She smiled enigmatically. 'I think we'd better just wait and see.'

The car had moved out of the prosperous part of the town and was now in the shanty fringes. Interspersed with palm trees were houses that were little more than shacks made of any kind of material that could be picked up for little or nothing. There were chickens, dogs and children everywhere, ragged washing hung on lines, open ditches doing the job of drains, flies, noise, laughter.

'This is the worst part of Portneuf,' the girl said. She sounded a little ashamed, on the defensive, as though she felt personally responsible for so much poverty and squalor.

Suddenly they were brought to a halt by a donkey and cart slewed across the road. The cart was loaded with sacks of vegetables, and an old, white-haired Negro with a face like a prune was sitting on the sacks, reins gripped in one hand and a long stick in the other. With the stick he was belabouring the donkey while cursing it in a high-pitched, indignant voice. The donkey just stood where it was, moving nothing but its ears, apparently unaffected either by blows or curses.

The girl drummed impatiently on the steering-wheel and a crowd of chattering, largely naked children gathered round the car and rubbed their fingers on the immaculate paintwork. Some men and women in patched cotton clothing looked on indifferently. The old man went on cursing and hitting the donkey. The donkey did not move; it stood with its head hanging, a picture of utter dejection and utter obstinacy.

10

'They do it to annoy you,' the girl said. She did not say whether she was referring to the donkey, the old Negro or the children. Perhaps she included all of them in the statement.

A very small boy was hanging on the door on Radford's side of the car. His head was just visible. He had wide, unwinking eyes and he stared at Radford as one might stare at a strange phenomenon never previously encountered. Radford felt a little uneasy under the gaze.

The man seemed to sprout suddenly from the ground. Radford had not seen him approach. He was tall and bony and his skin was the colour of coffee made with milk. He had a narrow face, the cheeks almost flat, and his nose was more aquiline than negroid. He was dressed in biscuit coloured trousers, a white shirt and suede shoes. The clothes seemed to be of far better quality than those of the other people near the car, and the man himself had the air of being in some way superior. He stood, slack-limbed, and looked at the girl with a trace of mockery in his expression.

'A little trouble, mademoiselle?'

She pressed her lips together. She did not look at him, did not answer.

'I could help perhaps — if asked.'

11

She said, still without looking at him: 'Will you move that cart?'

The man gave a laugh. 'It is not the most gracious way of asking. But no matter.'

He moved away from the car with a loose-limbed ease that contrived to be both graceful and faintly insolent. He grasped the donkey's bridle and forced it to move over to the side of the road.

'What do you mean, gran'pa, blocking the way. Don't you see that a fine young lady wishes to pass in her fine red car?'

The old Negro stopped cursing the donkey and grinned, revealing a toothless chasm of a mouth. The other man stood with one hand on the donkey's head, his back against the shafts of the cart, and signalled to the girl to drive on.

She took a coin from her handbag and tossed it to him. It landed at his feet and lay there. He did not attempt to pick it up. As the car went past he made a mock bow. The girl did not look at him.

Glancing back, Radford saw the man beckon one of the children. The child ran to him and picked up the coin. The man remained with his hand on the donkey, staring at the receding car.

'Who was he?' Radford asked.

'A mulatto.'

'It seemed to me that you knew him.'

'His name is Christophe — Georges Christophe. He is a labour leader, an agitator. Everybody in St Marien knows Christophe. He is notorious.'

'You don't like him?'

She answered coldly: 'I have no feelings whatever concerning him. He is of no importance to me.'

Radford did not pursue the subject. For some reason or other she seemed to be annoyed at having been obliged to accept help from Christophe. It was as though her pride had been injured by the necessity.

The car left the last ragged outskirts of the town. The road climbed gradually, winding between plantations of banana and citrus trees, past fields of sugar cane and along the steep sides of hills, green with vegetation. Here and there they passed mules or donkeys laden with panniers, and sometimes women with wide, shallow baskets balanced on their heads, walking barefooted with such natural grace and dignity that the baskets might have been golden crowns. Occasionally they passed a lorry or another car.

The girl had recovered her good humour. She said: 'How long is it since you saw Charles?'

Radford considered. 'Six or seven years.'

'You have never met Sophie, of course.'

'No. Charles was not married when I knew him.'

'You may find him changed.'

'We all change.'

She said musingly: 'We do not often have a guest. Perhaps not often enough. When my father was alive it was different. Charles is not a very sociable man.'

'Then he has certainly changed. At Oxford — '

'Oxford was a long time ago.'

The car turned right, leaving the highway and passing between a pair of high wrought-iron gates hinged to stone pillars. It was now on what was obviously a private road, white and dusty and a little grass growning between the wheel-tracks. This road followed a winding course between huge trees, the branches of which closed in overhead and made an avenue of shade from the sun.

They came upon the house suddenly, as one comes upon a picture in turning the pages of a book. It gave the instant impression of having grown naturally from the ground rather than of having been consciously designed and built. It was apparently not all of the same period, wings having been added to the original central core

14

of whitish stone. The roof was red-tiled and there were hinged shutters to the windows. On two sides of the house was a portico with stone columns and arches and vines trailing from arch to arch.

They left the car in front of the house and Radford followed the girl in under the portico and through a doorway into a spacious hall with a floor of coloured tiles, pleasantly cool after the heat outside. There was some dark, heavy furniture that looked as though it might have been mahogany or teak and numbers of thickly varnished pictures in tarnished gilt frames.

She saw him glance at the pictures.

'Ancestors. The Lamartines have been in St Marien a long time, you know.'

Doors and passages led off from the hall and along one side was a gallery with a stairway at one end. A woman appeared on the gallery, walked to the head of the stairs and descended slowly, one hand resting on the heavy banister rail. She was slender almost to thinness and her black hair fell almost to her shoulders and then turned in an upward sweep as though recoiling from the contact. Her face had a delicate beauty that seemed to have no need of cosmetic aid, but the skin was pale, suggesting that in this land of continual sunshine she kept always in the shadow.

Toni said in a low voice: 'My sister-in-law.' Then more loudly she added: 'Sophie, dear; here is Guy Radford.' Sophie Lamartine had reached the foot of the stairs. She walked towards them.

She said: 'I am so glad you have come. I have always wished to meet you.'

She did not look directly at him as she spoke. She seemed to be gazing at some point just to the left of him. He had forgotten until that moment that Charles had mentioned in a letter that his wife was blind.

2

An Offer

'You really haven't altered much in six years, Guy. You don't even look older, you lucky man.'

'I feel older,' Radford said.

He could have added, but did not, that six years had wrought considerable change in Lamartine. Charles had put on weight, a lot of it. He had a flabby look about him; there were pouches under his eyes, too much flesh beneath his chin.

There were five of them at dinner, seated at a polished mahogany table which would have comfortably accommodated three times the number. Besides Charles and his wife and Toni, there was Charles's mother, Nicolette Lamartine, a woman halfway between fifty and sixty, plump and blonde, but still maturely attractive. Radford had been introduced to her and she had said that she was happy to see him. She had added that she simply could not understand why anyone of his own free will should leave the civilization of Europe to come to such a primitive corner

17

of the world as St Marien.

'It has nothing whatever to recommend it, I assure you.'

'My mother has never ceased to regret leaving France,' Lamartine explained. 'My father went to Paris, fell in love with her at sight, married her and brought her back here. It was all very romantic.'

There was a trace of irony in his voice. Nicolette looked faintly annoyed, though she spoke lightly enough.

'One day I shall go back to Paris. I shall leave you children to your own devices.'

'When that time arrives,' Lamartine said, 'we shall have to do our best to bear the loss with what fortitude we are able to muster.'

The exchange had been bantering, half playful, but Radford sensed an undercurrent of something more. It might have been exaggeration to call it bitterness, but it was certainly not affection.

Two negro servants waited at table. They were both old; they seemed to be a part of the house, scarcely to be regarded as human beings but rather as automatons, robots designed merely for the purpose of obeying orders.

Nicolette pecked at her food without apparent pleasure. She said: 'I believe you are an engineer, Guy.'

'Of a sort.'

'If you're looking for a job,' Lamartine said, as though the idea had just come into his head, 'we could probably find you something at the mine.'

'The mine?'

Toni smiled in an I-told-you-so kind of way. 'Charles is chairman of the board of directors of the bauxite mining company.'

'Oh, I see.'

'It is always a good plan to have more than one interest,' Lamartine said. 'Sugar and coffee are unreliable. The market shifts so erratically. For aluminium there is always a keen demand.'

'And likely to be. Well, I might consider the offer if you're really serious about it.'

Lamartine smiled. 'It is one of the reasons why I invited you to come. Reliable men are difficult to find.'

Toni pouted. 'Guy is on holiday. I forbid you to put him to work in that disgusting mine.'

'The mine is not disgusting,' Lamartine said. 'But there is of course no hurry. Play first, work later, eh?'

Sophie had spoken very little. She was eating even less than the elder Madame Lamartine. She sat at the end of the table farthest from Charles and seemed to be outside the conversation, absorbed in her own thoughts. Perhaps, Radford thought, her blindness forced her into that situation.

He wondered whether she had always been blind or whether the affliction had come upon her after her marriage. Once or twice he tried to draw her into the circle, but she answered any remark that he made to her only briefly and seemed not to wish to become more deeply involved. Her voice was low and pleasant, and he noticed that her fingers manipulated the cutlery with no hint of clumsiness; it would have been impossible to guess that they were not being guided by normal sight.

Lamartine seemed for the most part to ignore her. She might have been simply another piece of furniture. When he did look at her it was with no evidence of affection; rather, to Radford's eyes, there appeared to be in his expression a suggestion of impatience, even of distaste. It needed no great powers of perception to see that if he had ever loved his wife that love no longer existed.

Lamartine said: 'You had a pleasant flight, I trust.'

'It would have been more pleasant if I had not been plagued by a man who sat next to me and talked too much.'

'Ah, you English,' Toni said. 'How you detest talking to strangers. Would you have had him sleep all the way?'

'Perhaps not. When he went to sleep he snored.'

'What was he like, this man?'

'He was fat and he wheezed. He said he was a salesman. His name was Blond.'

Lamartine stiffened in his chair. 'Did you say Blond?'

'Yes. Surely you don't know him?'

Lamartine fingered his wine glass, twisting it first one way, then the other. He seemed to be considering what answer to give to the question. Finally he said: 'I do know a man of that name who sells a certain type of machinery. If this is the same man and he has arrived in St Marien we may see him here. It is even possible that I may do some business with him.'

'With a fat man who wheezes?' Toni said. 'How depressing.'

'Do you have to talk such nonsense, Toni?' Lamartine spoke with sudden exasperation. For some reason or other the mention of Blond seemed to have put him out of humour. He drank more wine and fell silent.

'I have never been in an aeroplane,' Nicolette said. 'I should never dare to travel by air. I should be afraid of an accident.'

21

'Accidents occur on the ground too,' Radford said.

'That is true. Nevertheless — '

'Air lines have a very good record of safety, you know. I have just flown about six thousand kilometres and the first incident occurred after I had left the airport.'

'And what incident was that?' Nicolette did not seem deeply interested. She merely asked out of politeness.

'A donkey-cart stopped us on the road out of Portneuf. If a man named Christophe hadn't moved the donkey we might have been there still.'

He had told the story as an amusing anecdote, but the effect was not what he had expected. He could feel the sudden tension, the pause.

For a moment no one spoke. Then Lamartine said: 'Christophe, eh? So you have met Georges Christophe.'

'I have seen him.'

Lamartine turned to his sister. 'What did Christophe do? Tell me precisely everything that happened.'

She told him. Lamartine nodded. Radford could see that he was angry, though he tried to disguise the fact. Yet the incident had been so trivial, so unimportant. There seemed to be no reason for taking it so seriously.

'It was nothing. Nothing really.'

Lamartine looked at him with a sombre expression on his dark face. 'The thing in itself perhaps, yes. But you do not know this man. He is a devil, a very devil.'

It was, unexpectedly, Sophie who protested. 'No, Charles. You wrong him.'

He silenced her with a word. She winced as though he had struck her with his hand. She said no more.

A chandelier, converted to electricity, hung from the high ceiling. Light glinted on the cut glass and the silver. The table and sideboard had a dark, rich gleam that seemed to go deep into the wood. In this room, as in all the rest of the house, there was an aura of tradition. The Lamartines had been in St Marien for centuries. They had been slave-owners, and their way of life had changed little with the emancipation of the slaves. They were still the masters.

'This Christophe,' Lamartine said, and the name was ejected like some poisonous substance inadvertently allowed to get into the mouth. 'This Christophe is a menace to the prosperity and safety of St Marien. He ought to be behind bars — or, better still, removed altogether. If he is permitted to have his way the island will drift into anarchy and bloody revolution.'

'He did not look like a villain to me.'

Like his face, Lamartine's eyes were sombre. Seeing him thus, Radford remembered something he had forgotten — the strange moodiness that had always been a part of Charles's character. He remembered that their friendship had not been without its strains. In six years you tended to forget things like that; but they came back.

Lamartine said: 'You should not judge entirely by appearances. You will find much in St Marien that is not all it seems to be.'

A feeling of depression seemed to have invaded the room. Despite the richness, the solidity, Radford fancied he could detect a faint odour of decay. It might have been imagination.

Toni made an attempt to bring the talk round to a more cheerful theme. 'Tomorrow we must all go to St Clair.'

'St Clair?'

Lamartine explained quickly, as though glad to have had the subject changed: 'St Clair is our most fashionable holiday resort. It is on the north coast, the other side of the Blue Mountains. St Clair has everything — beaches, palms, hotels, splendid bathing. Also, of course, Americans. Very rich Americans.'

'It sounds fine.'

'Unfortunately, I shall not be able to go with you. There has been a little trouble at the mine. It is necessary for me to go up there tomorrow.'

For different reasons Nicolette and Sophie also excused themselves from the projected expedition, a fact which seemed neither to surprise Toni nor cause her any regret.

She said to Radford: 'Then you and I are the only two left. I forbid you to say that you have anything to prevent your going.'

'If there had been anything I should have put it aside,' Radford said. 'I can't think of a more delightful prospect than a visit to St Clair.'

Lamartine said: 'Another day I will show you the estate and the mine. But there is no hurry. Toni shall have you first.'

★   ★   ★

The room which had been allotted to Radford was large and the double bed looked strong enough to support an army. Yet here too he detected the subtle and indefinable odour of decay. It was as though the house had stood too long, held too many dark secrets, too many skeletons in cupboards.

Before undressing he lit a cigarette and walked to the window. Outside was a stone balcony enclosed by ornate wrought-iron railings. He stepped through the window and on to the balcony. Now that night had fallen it was considerably cooler, but not unpleasantly so.

There was a sliver of moon and he could see below him a drive leading to some outbuildings at the back of the house, and beyond the drive a dark mass of trees. A light wind was making the leaves rustle, and there were other sounds too — ticking, croaking, churring noises — audible evidence of all the vibrating activity that began with the descent of night.

Radford had been standing there only a few moments when he became aware of yet another sound. At first he had some difficulty in identifying it, but finally he was certain: it was the sound of a woman weeping.

There were other balconies on this side of the house and the sound of weeping appeared to be coming from the room on his left. Then he heard a voice, unmistakably Lamartine's, suppressed but clearly audible.

'Stop this nonsense, Sophie. It will do no good. Stop it, I say.'

The sound of the weeping continued.

'Very well,' Lamartine said. 'If you refuse to stop you must be made to.'

There followed a slight scuffling noise, a

faint cry, then silence.

Radford waited a little longer on the balcony, then threw his cigarette to the ground and went back into the bedroom. It was some considerable time before he fell asleep.

3

A Very Powerful Man

'You are very well tanned,' Toni said. 'I thought there was no sun in England. Nothing but rain and fog.'

Radford laughed. 'It's not quite as bad as that. The sun shines occasionally. But I got most of this overseas.'

The beach was powdered silver and palms grew almost to the water. The sea was a blue scimitar with an edge of white slicing at the land. Sun-worshippers lay on the sand or played in the water. Behind the palm trees the buildings of St Clair glittered like iced cakes.

'You have a fine body,' she said, looking at him with undisguised admiration.

'I could say the same about you.'

She answered frankly: 'It is quite perfect, isn't it?' She was wearing a bikini that left scarcely anything to the imagination. 'It would be so disgusting if I grew fat.'

'Why should you worry about growing fat?'

'You have seen my mother. In many ways I am like her — physically.'

'You'll have to watch the calories.'

She made a little wailing sound. 'But I love to eat.'

'Exercise moderation.'

'I have never been moderate.' She scooped up a handful of sand and let it trickle through her fingers. 'Do you intend to take the job Charles is offering?'

'I shall need to know more about it before deciding. At present it's all a little vague.'

'Would you have any objections to staying in St Marien? Making your home here?'

'There are attractions.'

He heard the sound of feet scuffing through the sand. A man's voice said: 'Well, my dear Toni. How delightful to see you.'

The man was dressed in gaily coloured shorts and a matching shirt, not buttoned. At first glance he gave an impression of youthfulness, but a closer inspection revealed that he was not so very young; there were flecks of grey in his black hair and rather deeper creases in his forehead and around his eyes than perhaps he himself cared to observe. Radford judged him to be not less than forty.

'Not working, Victor?' Toni said. There was no great warmth of greeting in her tone. One might have guessed that she would gladly have dispensed with the newcomer's presence.

If the man noticed any coldness in his reception, he took no notice. He sat down on the sand and his stomach bulged in folds over the waistband of his shorts. Black hair grew on all the visible parts of his body, on his arms, his legs, his chest, even on his back. He looked both soft and hard. The softness was in the excess of flesh that he carried, in a certain flabbiness; the hardness was in his eyes, in the set of his mouth.

'One must relax occasionally,' he said.

Toni introduced him perfunctorily. 'This is Victor Valland.'

Valland's eyes switched to Radford, seemed to weigh him up in one swift, calculating and extremely penetrating glance.

'And you, monsieur, are of course Guy Radford.'

Radford looked surprised. Valland laughed. 'In a community as small as this there are few secrets of any importance. One knows who comes and goes.'

'I think you make it your business to know,' Toni said. Then for Radford's information she added: 'Victor is one of the richest men in St Marien. I believe he has a finger in everything. Isn't that so, Victor?'

'My dear, you exaggerate of course. I am not so very rich,' Valland said. But the denial seemed merely formal; it carried no conviction.

He turned again to Radford. 'I understand that you may perhaps decide to stay here and work for the mining company.'

'You're jumping ahead,' Radford said. 'I haven't even had a firm offer yet.' He felt annoyed that Valland should apparently know so much of his business. He also resented the assessing manner in which Valland looked at him.

Valland said: 'I hope you decide to accept the offer when it does come. We need as many as possible on our side.'

'Your side?'

'The side of management and ownership.'

'The other side being, I take it, the workers?'

'Exactly. We do not want St Marien to go the way of Cuba. There is this fellow Christophe who might well see himself as another Castro.'

The girl broke in impatiently. 'Do we always have to talk about Christophe? Surely there are other subjects.'

Radford was intrigued by the way that name seemed to rouse her; the mention of it was like a needle thrust into her skin.

Valland appeared unsurprised. He smiled, as though in the outburst there were something that touched his sense of humour.

'As you wish, my dear. But let me tell you that Christophe is the man we must watch. We must watch him very carefully indeed.'

Driving home that evening, Toni suddenly asked: 'Has Charles told you how my father died?'

The question surprised Radford. 'No. Is it important?'

'He was murdered.'

For a moment he did not react to the word. It had been spoken without emphasis; she might in the same tone have told him that Pierre Lamartine had died of a heart attack or a fever. But murder was something different; though delayed, the impact came.

'Murdered?'

'Exactly. And I think it is best that you should learn the facts from me or Charles, and Charles seems unwilling to tell you. Sooner or later you would be bound to hear something and you might get a mangled account of what really happened.'

'Was the murderer caught?' Radford asked.

'He was caught and executed. But the others went free.'

'What others?'

'The ones who paid him to do what he did.'

'I'm afraid I don't understand,' Radford

said. 'If you really want to tell me about it, it might be best to start at the beginning.'

She was silent for a moment. Then she said: 'There isn't a lot to tell. It happened one evening. We were all at home. A man came to the door. He told the servant he had a message for my father. He refused to come in. My father went to the door and somehow the man persuaded him to go outside. We don't know how he did it, but no doubt he had prepared some plausible story to entice my father away from the house. Anyway, my father went with him and never came back. His body was found later less than a hundred paces away.'

She paused. Radford said nothing. He waited for her to go on. After a few moments she did so.

'He had been brutally murdered. You know what a machete is? The big knife that's used for cutting sugar cane.'

'I know,' Radford said. 'It's rather like the parang used in Malaya. A nasty weapon.'

'There was a machete lying beside my father's body. It was covered with blood. My father was almost unrecognizable. The man must have struck him a hundred times.'

'And you say the man was found?'

'Of course. Our servant had seen him and recognized him. The machete was identified.

It belonged to a labourer named Anton Giraud, a mulatto. This was the man our servant had seen at the door. Giraud did not even attempt to deny the crime. It would have been useless anyway; the evidence against him was overwhelming.'

'Didn't he try to escape?'

'Oh, yes. He fled into the mountains. But it did not take the police long to catch him.'

'And then he was tried and executed?'

'Yes.'

'Did he explain why he had killed your father?'

'He told a lot of lies which I will not repeat. But he was a very stubborn man. Until the very end he still maintained that no one else had been involved in the crime. What nonsense. Anyone with the least claim to intelligence could see that it was a political murder.'

'What makes you say that?'

'My father was one of the most influential men in this country. He was implacably opposed to communism in all its forms. That is why he wished to have President Petra deposed.'

'But Petra isn't a communist, surely.'

'He is a liberal — and perhaps that is worse.'

'How long is it since this happened?' Radford asked.

'Six months. Some people may have forgotten. Others do not forget so easily.' She searched in her handbag for cigarettes, lit two and handed one to Radford. 'This is a gloomy subject. Let's talk of something else.'

But it was difficult to recapture the former lighthearted mood. They both tried, but for the rest of the journey conversation was disjointed and fragmentary. The shadow of the dead man seemed to have fallen upon them and would not go. It was a relief when they reached the house and saw light streaming from the windows.

'Home,' said Toni. She sounded glad to be back. There were several other cars standing in front of the house.

'You have visitors,' Radford said.

'Yes. Charles told me there was to be a meeting of the Association this evening.'

'Association?'

'Of employers. Landowners, mine directors. They discuss business and drink rum and play cards. It's chiefly social.' She seemed to regret having mentioned the Association and to be trying to dismiss it as a matter of little importance.

They went into the house. From one of the rooms that opened off the big hall came the sound of voices, a sudden gust of laughter. The door opened and Radford had a view of men getting up from chairs; of a long table such as might be found in a boardroom, of bottles and glasses and a thick haze of tobacco smoke. He could see no playing cards.

Valland came out of the room, talking to a dandified man scarcely bigger than a midget. He caught sight of Toni and Radford and guided his companion towards them.

'So I got here before you. I hope you had an enjoyable day.'

'Very enjoyable,' Toni said with an emphasis that surprised Radford.

Valland turned to Radford. 'I don't think you have met Monsieur Porchaire. Felix, this is Monsieur Radford from England.'

Porchaire held out a hand. When he gripped it Radford had a curious feeling that he was shaking hands with a puppet. Porchaire was perfection in miniature. He was dressed in a beautifully cut grey lightweight suit; his shirt was pale blue and his tie dark blue; the tie was impaled by a gold pin in which one large emerald glowed as though with an inner fire. Had he been just a little bigger, Monsieur Porchaire might have been called handsome; as it was he succeeded only in looking faintly ludicrous. He was

36

perhaps fifty years old and his voice was an incongruously powerful bass.

'I am most pleased to make your acquaintance, Monsieur Radford. Charles has already spoken to me about you. I hope we may be able to persuade you to join us. We need young men of ability.'

He bowed slightly and moved away with Valland. He was wearing crocodile leather shoes and he walked with little mincing steps, as though at any moment he might break into a run.

'Felix is a director of the mining company — as well as nearly every other company in St Marien,' Toni explained. 'He is a very powerful man.'

'He doesn't look very powerful.'

'You mustn't be deceived by his appearance. He and Victor and Charles between them might be said to control the economy of St Marien.'

'It's a funny thing,' Radford said. 'I was under the impression that I came here for a holiday, but everybody seems to be in a conspiracy to make me work.'

'I'm not,' Toni said. 'Not yet.'

Charles Lamartine and half a dozen other men had now come out into the hall. There was only one man left in the room in which the meeting had taken place. This man was still seated at the table, comfortably smoking a cigar and making no move to leave. He glanced towards the door and saw Radford looking at him. He gave a small nod of the head and smiled. He was plump and middle-aged and he had thin brown hair plastered down with cream. He was Monsieur Henri Blond, the machinery salesman.

4

The Mine

There were five of them at breakfast — Lamartine and his wife, Toni, Monsieur Blond and Radford. Nicolette was remaining in her room, a fact which appeared to cause no surprise to her son and daughter.

'Monsieur Blond will be staying for a few days,' Lamartine said. 'We have a considerable amount of business to get through and it will be more convenient.'

Sophie Lamartine said nothing, but Radford thought he detected a slight compression of the lips. He guessed that she had not been consulted on the matter.

Blond smiled ingratiatingly. 'It is most kind of you to permit the imposition. I am greatly obliged. Indeed, yes.' He lifted his coffee cup and drank with a clearly audible sucking noise. His eyes peered over the cup, watchful, calculating. He might have been measuring the possibilities of each person at the table as a potential customer.

Toni said: 'Do you always work in this part of the world, Monsieur Blond?'

Blond shook his head. 'But no. I have worked in a great many different countries, both in Europe and America. I go wherever there is money to be made.'

'That is your only interest?'

'Not the only interest, no. But one must live.'

'I think,' Lamartine said, 'that that is a necessity not universally shared.' He looked at Blond with an enigmatic smile twitching the corners of his mouth. 'Would you not agree?'

Blond began to laugh softly. The laughter made his chin tremble. If there was really a joke it was shared only by him and Lamartine; no one else was taking any part in it.

Blond's laughter died as suddenly as it had begun. He said: 'I understand you perfectly, monsieur. But yes, quite perfectly.'

Lamartine turned to Radford. 'Monsieur Blond and I are going to the mine this morning. If you have nothing more urgent to do it might interest you to go with us.'

'I'd like it,' Radford said.

Toni pouted. 'Are you tired of my company so soon?'

'I thought you would be in the party too.'

Lamartine gave a laugh. 'I see that you are a diplomat as well as an engineer. That is a valuable combination. Well, Toni, do you wish to come?'

She made a grimace. 'Mines do not interest me. And besides, I have seen it before. I shall go to Portneuf and buy a pair of shoes.'

'You are always going to Portneuf to buy shoes.'

'That is a ridiculous statement.'

'If it is not shoes it is something else — stockings, hats, dresses — '

'It needn't worry you. It's my money.'

'True,' Lamartine said. 'I sometimes forget that you are a woman of independent means.'

He let the subject drop.

★ ★ ★

They travelled to the mine in Lamartines's blue Mercedes. Blond had a hired car, a three-years-old Citroen, but they left this at the house and all three climbed into the Mercedes, Blond in the back.

They drove past orchards of citrus trees and fields of sugar cane taller than a man. In places black labourers were cutting the cane with machetes and loading it on to lorries or mule carts. Some of them stared at the blue car as it went past, the machetes hanging loosely at their sides. To Radford they seemed to be without expression. If they resented the

41

contrast between the opulent car and their own wretched clothing, ragged, patched and bleached from much washing and drying in the sun, they gave no sign. They stood like patient animals; and yet, under the surface, there might have been some current stirring. Castro had shown the way in Cuba. It could happen here.

'How much land do you own, monsieur?' Blond asked, sitting forward on the rear seat.

Lamartine answered carelessly, as though it were a matter of small importance: 'Ten thousand hectares. Perhaps more.'

Blond made a soft hissing noise with his lips. 'So much! It is a large stake for a man to have in the world.'

'It is enough to fight for.'

'But yes.' Blond was silent for a while; then he said in a ruminative way: 'For myself I think I shall never own more than two metres by one — and even that I shall not live to enjoy.'

★   ★   ★

The mine was a great red wound in the side of the hill. Bulldozers and mechanical shovels had torn away vegetation and surface soil and had bitten deep into the clay from which the alumina was extracted. On each side of the

42

working rugged cliffs rose to a height more than a hundred feet. Trees and shrubs grew on the tops of these cliffs and their roots could be seen apparently searching for a foothold that was no longer there.

'Is it all opencast?' Radford asked.

'No,' Lamartine said. 'We go underground too.'

They came to a cluster of huts, timber-walled, iron-roofed.

'Most of the workers live on the site,' Lamartine explained. 'The company lets the houses at a fixed-rent. It is taken out of their wages.'

Houses seemed to Radford a flattering description for such dwellings, but he made no remark. At worst they were better than many of the buildings he had seen on the fringes of Portneuf.

A railway track ran into the mine and steel trucks were being loaded from a chute fed by mechanical shovels. There was a constant noise of labouring engines and clanging metal. The air was hot and humid. Radford could feel his clothes sticking to him. Blond was sweating freely.

'Where do you send the bauxite?' Radford asked.

'We have a processing plant on the Varne on the outskirts of Portneuf. We transport the bauxite there by our own railway and then extract the alumina. Two kilos of bauxite yield one kilo of alumina.'

'And the alumina?'

'It is shipped to Canada for final processing. We do not make any aluminium in St Marien. We do not have the necessary electrical power.'

They left the car and went forward on foot. Set some distance away from the dwelling huts was a large building with a painted signboard on which it was possible to read: 'Compagnie Minérale de St Marien'.

The door was open. Lamartine went inside and the two others followed.

There was not much furniture — a few desks, steel filing cabinets, plain wooden chairs. Some dark-skinned clerks were busy at the desks. Under the corrugated iron roof the hut's interior was like a furnace.

Lamartine ignored the clerks, who, after one furtive glance, remained sedulously engrossed in their work. He crossed to a door on the right which had frosted glass in the upper half. He did not trouble to knock, but turned the handle and went into an inner office where an electric fan lazily stirred the air without making it noticeably cooler. He beckoned to Radford and Blond to follow, and they also walked in.

This inner room was more comfortably furnished than the outer one, but the difference was not great. Radford closed the door. The fan made a thin squeaking noise as though timidly protesting against overwork.

A man got up from the desk at which he had been working. He was almost white, but there was a trace of Negro in him. He was lean and his face was pockmarked. He could have been forty-five, possibly more.

'Good day, Maurice,' Lamartine said.

'Good day, monsieur.'

Lamartine introduced the man to Radford and Blond. 'Maurice Baraud is our mine manager. He has been with us now for — how many years is it, Maurice?'

'Twenty-eight, monsieur.'

'Not always as manager, of course. He worked his way up. He is devoted to the company's interests. Isn't that so, Maurice?'

'Yes, monsieur.'

Baraud looked slightly hunted. The discussion of himself in front of strangers seemed to embarrass him.

Blond said: 'Devotion is not always easy to find in these days.' He smiled, as though mildly amused by it all.

Lamartine walked to the window of the office and looked out. From the window a part of the mine was visible. One could see

45

machines working. The noise of them came across in a continuous muffled roar like the sound of wild animals.

Lamartine spoke without turning. 'Have you anything to report, Maurice?'

'To report, monsieur?'

'Anything of particular interest.'

'No, monsieur.' There had been perhaps a momentary hesitation before the answer. 'Nothing.'

'No unrest among the men?'

Baraud looked uncomfortable. The question seemed to worry him. He answered with some reluctance, as though forced into the admission against his will.

'There is some grumbling about pay. The men think they are not getting a fair wage. The cost of living has risen steeply. It is difficult to buy the necessities — '

Lamartine said coldly: 'You are talking like a union agitator. Whose side are you supporting?'

'I am only telling you what the men are saying, monsieur.'

'They are always discontented. If we doubled their wages they would come again within a month asking for more. How long do you imagine the company would last if it gave in to all the demands of these — these animals?'

46

Baraud was silent. The hunted look in his eyes was more apparent than ever. There were lines of strain about his mouth.

Lamartine turned. He laughed. 'Maurice, Maurice, you are too tender-hearted. You listen too much to the complaints of these creatures. You pay too much attention to their lies.'

'I do not think it is all lies, monsieur.'

'Their exaggerations then. Don't you see that they are bound to complain? In that way they hope to get more for themselves. It is the way of things. They are lucky to have regular employment. There are many in St Marien who are not so fortunate. Is that not so?'

'Yes, monsieur. There is much unemployment.'

'So.'

Lamartine turned again to gaze out of the window.

The fan squeaked rhythmically and a big black spider scurried across the floor. Blond, with surprising swiftness for so plump a man, put out his foot and crushed the spider. Radford could hear the crunching noise as the creature collapsed under Blond's shoes.

Blond wiped the sole on the wooden floor of the office and left a dark, sticky smear on the boards. He looked down at it with an expression of gloating satisfaction on his large, moist face. Radford also looked at the remains of the spider and then at Blond. He experienced a feeling of revulsion, not so much at the death of the spider but at the manner of its destruction. Blond had so obviously enjoyed the slaughter.

Lamartine, still with his back to the room, said: 'There is a mechanical shovel not working. Why is that?'

'It is out of action,' Baraud said.

Lamartine's voice was icy. 'Give me credit for being able to observe that much with my own eyes. Why is it out of action?'

'The gear-box, monsieur.' Baraud sounded intensely unhappy. 'A breakage. There was, it appears, no oil.'

Lamartine turned and stared at Baraud. 'Who was responsible for seeing that there was oil in the gearbox?'

'Jean Dessine, monsieur.'

'And this — Jean Dessine — what action have you taken regarding him?'

'I have reprimanded him, monsieur.'

'You have reprimanded him!' Lamartine's expression was one of utter amazement. 'A man, by reason of criminal negligence, puts out of action a piece of machinery costing forty thousand fontaines, and you reprimand him. Are you quite certain that you did not congratulate him?'

'It was an oversight, monsieur. He was worried about his wife. She is sick and there are five children — five of them. I am sure it will not happen again.'

'It will certainly not happen again, because you will discharge him — as you should have done at once.'

Baraud seemed to be in torment. 'But, monsieur, his wife, his five children — '

'Let us get this clear,' Lamartine said in a hard, cold voice. 'I am not concerned with the private affairs of inefficient employees. I am concerned solely with the economical running of this mine, do you understand? This fellow Dessine has sabotaged a valuable machine which we can ill spare — '

'It can be repaired, monsieur.'

'Of course it can be repaired. And what will it cost? How much will the loss of its use for days, possibly weeks, take from the profits of the company? All this through the carelessness of one man. Sentiment cannot be allowed to enter into the matter. In cases such as this an example must be made. You will see to it without further delay.'

'Yes, monsieur.'

They went out of the hut and the sun struck at them like a copper lance. Blond mopped his face.

'It is hot.'

'It is always hot,' Lamartine said. 'One gets accustomed to it. Come, I will show you round the mine.'

Baraud had come too. He walked a few paces behind, with them and yet not of them, separated by a vast intangible gulf.

Wherever they went the mine-workers glanced at them and recognized Lamartine, and if they had been smiling before or singing they became on the instant sullen and silent. It was impossible not to sense the antagonism; it was like a cloud following them.

Here and there narrow gauge rails carried lines of small tipper trucks that disappeared into the entrances of underground workings or came out loaded with ore. This was the basic material from which some day might spring a kettle, a saucepan, a car, an aeroplane, even a house. The uses of aluminium were wide, the demand insatiable. Lamartine had a solid basis for his prosperity, even ignoring the estate. He should have been a happy man; yet he did not look happy.

As they drove away from the mine Radford glanced back and saw Baraud standing motionless, watching the receding car and thinking perhaps of the unpleasant duty of dismissing an employee whose negligence had put out of action a piece of expensive machinery — thinking about it and not liking it.

'Maurice is too weak,' Lamartine said. 'I think he may have to be replaced.'

'You said he was devoted to the company's interests,' Radford said. He felt sorry for Baraud.

'Devotion is not enough. One needs a certain toughness of character. In Maurice I fear that toughness is lacking.'

'So you will remove him? Just like that?'

'It may be necessary — when a replacement is ready.'

'It will be a blow to Baraud. What will he do?'

'That will be his concern, not mine. As I have said before, one cannot allow sentiment to affect a matter of business. If a man is inefficient or obstructive, if he is in any way an obstacle to success, he must be removed. The principle applies in every case — and is not confined to industry. It applies to those at the top just as much as those at the bottom, to a president as surely as to a labourer.'

He paused, then added in a softly musing tone that yet had in it a hint of steel: 'Perhaps most of all to a president, since his influence for good or ill is so much greater than another man's.'

From the back of the car Radford heard a kind of panting like old, wheezy bellows at work. It was the sound of Blond chuckling.

5

Invitation

'I have an appointment at my hairdresser's,' Toni said. 'Would you like to come into Portneuf with me? You will have to amuse yourself for an hour or two.'

'I think I can manage to do that,' Radford said. 'I haven't really had a look at Portneuf yet.'

'When they have finished my hair I will take you on a conducted tour.'

'That sounds fine.'

It was the day after the visit to the mine. Lamartine had gone off early on some estate business, taking Blond with him. Blond appeared to be in no hurry to leave and seemed to be taking his work very lightly. Radford wondered just what it was he was selling, but the question did not greatly bother him. He found Monsieur Blond rather a bore, a dull, fat man who ate too much and seemed to be permanently enjoying some exquisite private joke.

Toni thought Blond was rather unpleasant. 'Like a big shiny slug. I should hate to be touched by him. I can't understand why Charles has him here. But then Charles explains nothing. He does just as he pleases without consulting anyone.'

She parked the car in a side street near the hairdresser's and left Radford to his own devices.

'Meet me here in two hours. And don't be late.' He promised to be punctual and set out on a leisurely stroll. Almost at once he came upon the Place Fontaine, a paved square set round with palm trees and having in the centre a marble statue of the Liberator. Albert La Fontaine was standing, sword in hand, with one foot on the chest of a fallen French soldier and was surrounded by fountains made in the shape of mermaids and dolphins. In St Marien you could never long escape from some reminder of the man to whom the island owed its liberty. Even the unit of currency, equivalent to some two shillings in value, was named after him, and it was his image and not that of any succeeding president that appeared on stamps and coinage.

Radford was reading the inscription on the plinth of Fontaine's statue when he heard his name spoken by a man's voice. Turning, he saw a mulatto whose face seemed familiar but which did not immediately identify itself in his mind.

'You have forgotten me,' the man said. He had a narrow face and there was a hint of laughter in the eyes.

'No,' Radford said, remembering an incident with a donkey. 'You are Georges Christophe.'

'So they told you. I thought perhaps they would not.'

'Why?'

'Monsieur Radford, I do not think you are a fool. You must surely realize that I am not loved by Charles or Antoinette Lamartine.'

Christophe was smiling; he seemed to find something faintly amusing in the situation. Today he was wearing a blue shirt only partly buttoned, so that it was possible to see a triangle of brown chest, smooth and hairless, below the muscular neck. He looked lithe and strong; he would not have been out of place at an athletics meeting. Nor was he unhandsome in a lean hard way. The strange thing was that Radford had an impression of having seen Christophe somewhere before, not simply on the day of his arrival in St Marien but even earlier. There was something vaguely familiar about the man, but it could have been an illusion. Nevertheless it troubled Radford slightly because he could not pin it down.

'How did you know my name?' he asked.

Christophe lifted his shoulders in an expressive gesture. 'It is general knowledge in Portneuf. Monsieur Lamartine is a man of importance. If he has a guest everyone is curious to know who that guest may be. The news goes around. We know also of Monsieur Blond.'

'And does your knowledge extend to the nature of Monsieur Blond's business?'

'We know that he is supposed to be a salesman. It would interest us to know just what kind of goods he is selling.'

'I understand it is machinery.'

'Ah, yes, but what type of machinery?'

'You'll have to ask somebody else for the answer to that question. I don't know any more than you do.'

'Perhaps some day you will find out. Perhaps then you may feel inclined to give me the information.'

Radford gave a laugh, half amused, half resentful. Christophe appeared to be presuming a great deal on a very slender acquaintance.

'I see no reason why I should give you any information.'

Christophe was not put out. He said: 'When you have the information perhaps you will see the reason.' He looked up at the

56

statue of Fontaine but there was no admiration in his expression. 'The glorious liberator. Albert La Fontaine, I salute you.' He made a mock bow and turned away.

He had walked only a few paces when he stopped and came back. 'Monsieur Radford,' he said. 'May I give you a word of advice?'

'If you wish.'

'Do not accept Lamartine's offer.'

'I don't know what you're talking about.'

'I am talking about the position he is offering you — at the mine. Be wise, monsieur. Do not accept it. Be even more wise and go home. St Marien is not the place for you. It is an angry island.'

Radford was nettled by the impudence of the man. He said: 'I shall please myself when I leave St Marien, and if Monsieur Lamartine should offer any kind of post I shall decide for myself whether or not to accept it. I require no advice from you or from anyone else on how to arrange my own affairs.'

Christophe grinned. 'I understand, monsieur. No man of spirit cares to be told what to do. But remember what I have said. It is for your own good, believe me.'

Christophe was looking at Radford with a quizzical expression. He said: 'If you are not too busy, monsieur, we might have a little talk, eh?'

'On what subject?'

'Should we say on the subject of the internal affairs of St Marien?'

'I am looking round Portneuf.'

'I will show you what is interesting. And we will talk as we go.'

'Very well.'

It had to be admitted that Christophe was an excellent guide. He obviously knew every inch of Portneuf, had studied its history and could talk interestingly and even wittily about it. Somehow it was difficult to see in him the ogre that Charles and Toni Lamartine had painted. Many people greeted him as they walked, and he had a smile and a word for all; sometimes a question regarding family matters, sometimes a joke, sometimes merely a friendly wave of the hand.

'You are well known,' Radford said.

'It is not surprising. I am general secretary of the workers' union.'

'Which union?'

'In St Marien there is only one. The stevedores, the plantation hands, the miners, the truck drivers, all belong to the same one. Once there were dozens of petty unions, none of which had any power; now there is only one and it has much power. It is better that way.'

'And the government allows an amalgamation like that to take place?'

'President Petra is a good man. He is neither an industrialist nor a landowner; he is an academic. That is why the capitalists would like to be rid of him. They will never be able to do so by constitutional means because the President is too well loved; he has the backing of the people.'

'You think other ways of removing him may be tried?'

'It is possible,' Christophe said.

★ ★ ★

The President's Palace was a white stone building that owed something to the architecture of ancient Greece — the tall columns, the wide steps, the classic lines. In front was a forecourt protected by stout iron railing, the gates guarded by sentries in colourful uniforms of blue and scarlet cloth with white helmets on their heads. The bayonets on the sentries' rifles flashed in the sun.

'The Palace has been stormed several times,' Christophe said. 'There are bullet marks in the stone.'

There was a car standing at the foot of the steps within the forecourt. It was a white

59

Rolls-Royce with a small blue and yellow flag of the Republic of St Marien mounted on the radiator. A man came down the steps and got into the car, and as it drove away an escort of motor cyclists joined it.

As this small procession swept towards the main gate and out into the square Radford could see the man who had come from the Palace sitting in the back of the Rolls-Royce. He was a small man and he was bareheaded. His hair was white and he had a thin face, deeply lined. A few people who were standing nearby waved their hats in salutation; a woman shouted something; it might have been a blessing.

The man in the car inclined his head slightly in recognition of the salutes, and then the Rolls-Royce with its escort of motor cycles receded in the distance and was lost to sight.

'That was President Petra,' Christophe said. 'The car has bullet-proof glass of course.'

They left the Palace Square and the sun poured down its heat from a cloudless sky. There was a sound of a ship's siren, the thunder of jet engines as an air-liner circled the airport before coming in to land, the hooting of cars.

'I should like you to see my home,'

Christophe said, 'if you would not object to such a visit.'

'Why should I object?'

'To be seen going to my house might compromise you in certain quarters.'

'I'm not afraid of being compromised,' Radford said, 'but my time is running short.' He glanced at his watch. 'I have to meet Mademoiselle Lamartine for lunch in half an hour.'

'Another time then?'

'Yes, another time.'

'Perhaps you would care to come tomorrow evening. I am free then. We have not talked of anything important.' He seemed very eager that Radford should agree to the proposal. It was as though, like the Ancient Mariner, he felt a need to tell some story.

'I don't know,' Radford said. 'I have no car and I don't think I could ask one of the Lamartines to drive me into Portneuf.'

'I will come and fetch you.'

Radford thought the matter over. He felt certain that it would not please either Toni or Charles if he were to go to Christophe's house, but he was curious to hear what the union leader had to say. Finally he made up his mind to accept the invitation and risk the displeasure of his hosts.

'Thank you then. I shall be pleased to come.'

When he told Toni about the proposed visit she stared at him as though she thought he had gone out of his mind.

'You can't mean it. You must be joking.'

'Why should I make a joke like that? It isn't funny, is it?'

'No,' she said; 'no, it's not funny at all. Do you realize what you are proposing to do?'

'Of course. To go and have a talk with Christophe in his own home. It should be interesting.'

'Oh, yes, certainly it will be interesting.' There was suppressed anger in her voice. If it had not been for the other people in the restaurant he believed she would have shouted at him. As it was, she kept her voice low, but just how angry she was showed in the twist of her mouth and the glitter of her eyes. 'So you really intend to go and listen to the lies he has to tell?'

'Why should he tell me any lies?'

'Because he is — '

'Is what?'

'Because he is Christophe.'

'That hardly seems a sufficient reason.'

A waiter came with coffee; it was the colour of his skin. His starched white jacket made a vivid contrast. He served the coffee and went away. Air conditioning made the restaurant comfortably cool. There was a gleam of silver and glass and chromium plate.

'Charles will not be pleased.'

'I don't see why he should object.'

'Christophe is laughing at us. He is using you as a pawn.'

'Don't you think you are being slightly ridiculous?'

She froze at once. 'I think we had better go. I have to get back home.'

'You were going to take me on a conducted tour of Portneuf. Have you forgotten?'

'I think that is hardly necessary now. You appear to have had a different guide.'

⋆ ⋆ ⋆

At dinner it was obvious that Toni had not yet thrown off her ill temper. Lamartine rallied his sister. 'What is wrong with you?' He glanced at Radford. 'Ah, I see what it is. You and Guy went into Portneuf and had an argument. Is that so?'

She made no answer. She merely looked down at the table, but Radford could see the colour rising in her cheeks.

Lamartine gave a laugh. 'You must not take this seriously, my dear Guy. Toni is given to these moods. Tomorrow she will have forgotten what the argument was about.'

Toni raised her head and spoke angrily. 'You talk like a fool, Charles. I shall not have forgotten. It was about Christophe.'

Lamartine stopped smiling. There was a complete change in his voice; it was no longer bantering.

'In what way — about Christophe?'

'He has invited Guy to visit him at his home.'

'The impudence of the fellow. The infernal impudence.'

'That is not all.'

'Not all?' The meaning of this statement seemed gradually to dawn on him. He stared at Radford unbelievingly. 'You are not seriously thinking of accepting the invitation.'

'I have already accepted,' Radford said.

Nicolette began to giggle. Radford glanced at her and came to the conclusion that she had been drinking. It was not the first occasion on which he had suspected that she was inclined to take more from the bottle than was good for her. He had a shrewd idea now what the complaint was to which Toni had referred and which had nothing to do with the climate.

Lamartine said in a low, furious voice: 'Stop that, Mother. Stop it!'

His words had an immediate effect.

Nicolette stopped giggling and controlled herself with an obvious effort. She contrived to look unnaturally grave and began to toy with the food on her plate without however actually eating anything.

Blond looked amused. He went on eating with as much enjoyment as ever, but his eyes missed nothing.

'You cannot be serious,' Lamartine said. 'You don't really intend to go to Christophe's home.'

'Certainly I do. Is there any reason why I should not?'

'But it's unthinkable. That a guest of mine should fraternize with a person of that description! Can you imagine what effect such an act may have? What kind of talk there will be?'

'Are you afraid of what people will say?' Radford asked in surprise. 'I thought that kind of reaction was a thing of the past.'

'Perhaps in St Marien we live in the past.'

'In Jamaica — '

'St Marien is not Jamaica.'

'I am beginning to realize that. Look, Charles, I'm sorry if this isn't to your liking, but I've already told Christophe I'll go and I don't see any reason to break that promise.'

Lamartine appeared about to make an angry reply, but controlled himself and said in a milder tone: 'Suppose I were to ask you, as a friend, not to go.'

Radford considered this. It was a stronger argument than any threat could have been, and probably Lamartine realized this. But the very fact that both Charles and Toni were so set against his visiting Christophe made him all the keener to go. And it was so unreasonable not to. Public opinion could not be as important as that. Nevertheless, it had to be admitted that, as a guest, he owed some consideration to the wishes of his hosts, however ridiculous those wishes might seem.

He was still hesitating over the answer when Sophie unexpectedly broke the silence. She said: 'I think Guy should please himself whether or not he goes. He is a guest, not a prisoner.'

There was a momentary hush after this remark. Even Blond stopped eating, but the faint smile was still on his face as his glance travelled from Lamartine to Sophie and back again to Lamartine. He seemed to be waiting, and perhaps hoping, for an outburst; but the outburst did not come.

Instead, Lamartine said in an ice-cold voice: 'No one asked for your opinion, Sophie. I should be obliged if you would not interfere in matters that are no concern of yours.'

Radford saw two red spots appear in Sophie's cheeks and a compression of the lips, but there was no other reaction. He felt a sudden impulse to strike Lamartine, but he resisted the impulse.

'I shall go to Christophe's,' he said.

Blond stroked his plump chin and smiled broadly. Nicolette began to giggle again. This time no one stopped her.

6

A Different Story

Christophe was standing in the portico when Radford went out. He had not been invited to wait in the house.

Night fell at about six o'clock in St Marien and it was already dark. Christophe's car was standing in the drive; it was a rather battered Simca.

'Not very new,' Christophe said, 'but it serves my purpose. I don't have to keep up appearances. If I ran an expensive car questions might be asked. After all, it is the union members who pay for it and many of them can't even afford a bicycle.'

He let in the clutch and they moved away from the house. Christophe was wearing a dark blue suit and an open-necked shirt; he was bareheaded and there was a signet ring on the third finger of his left hand. He glanced at Radford.

'You did not change your mind then.'

'Did you expect me to change it?'

'I thought they would try to persuade you not to come.'

'And you thought I would be open to persuasion?'

'Who is not, monsieur?'

The sky was dusted with stars and myriads of insects were caught in the white beams of the headlights. The Simca ran smoothly despite its age.

'Have you found out what it is Monsieur Blond is selling?' Christophe asked.

'I haven't troubled to inquire. It doesn't interest me very greatly.'

'Perhaps it should.'

'Do you have to talk in riddles?'

'If I talk in riddles it is only because I myself do not know the answer.'

'And you are interested?'

'I am very interested.'

* * *

Christophe's house was in the western suburbs of Portneuf. It was built of timber, with a verandah on stilts at the front and steps leading up to it. The front door was under the verandah, which acted as a porch. There was a small garden enclosed by a palisaded fence and the evening air was fragrant with the scent of flowers.

They went into a cramped entrance hall which was little more than a passage with doors opening from it on each side. Two children, a boy and a girl, scarcely five years old, rushed at Christophe with squeals of delight, then saw Radford and stopped, abashed.

Christophe laughed. 'Don't be shy now. Monsieur Radford is not an ogre to frighten little children. Josette, Jacques, come and shake hands.'

The children came forward and shook hands solemnly with Radford. They were a shade darker than Christophe but it was easy to see he was their father.

Christophe bent down and kissed them, the girl first, the boy second.

'Where is your mother?'

The girl answered. She was the older of the two. 'In the kitchen.'

Christophe went to a door on the left and opened it. 'Will you come in here, monsieur?'

Radford went into the room. It was quite small. There were some armchairs and a settee, a table littered with papers, a general impression of untidiness and comfort. It looked like a room that was lived in.

The children had followed, staring at Radford with open curiosity.

Christophe said: 'If you will wait here a moment, monsieur — ' He turned and good-humouredly hustled the children out of the room. 'Time little people were in bed, I think.'

Radford was not left alone for long. Christophe came back with a woman whom he introduced as his wife. Marie Christophe was rather plump, with a round, pleasant face and a mass of black hair tightly curled.

'I'm glad you could come, Monsieur Radford. Georges has told me about you.'

'Nothing bad, monsieur, I assure you,' Christophe said.

Radford laughed. 'I don't doubt it. You don't know anything bad — yet. And won't you drop the monsieur and just call me Guy?'

'If you will call me Georges.' He turned to his wife. 'Marie, would you get some beer?'

She went out of the room and came back with some cans of beer and two glasses. Moisture was condensing on the cans, indicating that they had come out of a refrigerator.

'You would like a glass of beer?'

'Very much,' Radford said.

Christophe punctured the cans and poured two glasses. He handed one to Radford and took the other one himself.

'Marie doesn't drink beer. She thinks it would ruin her figure.' He laughed. Marie laughed. Their good humour was infectious. Radford was glad he had come.

After a few minutes Marie excused herself. 'I must see the children into bed and prepare the supper. You will stay to supper?'

'If it is not too much bother,' Radford said.

'You would offend her if you refused,' Christophe said. 'And you are quite safe. Marie is a wonderful cook.'

'I'm sure of it.'

As soon as his wife had left the room Christophe became more serious. 'I wonder,' he said, 'what Monsieur Lamartine has told you about me.'

'Why should you think he has told me anything?'

'Oh, he is bound to have done so. But you needn't tell me if it embarrasses you. I can guess. He has probably told you that I am a rogue, a liar and a trouble-maker. Ah, I see by your expression that I have hit the mark. Well, it does not worry me. I am used to hard words.'

'He seems to think you are out to ruin the mine.'

'Which is, of course, ridiculous. How would that help the union? On the contrary, I wish the mine to prosper. All I am trying to do is to obtain better pay and better working conditions for my members.'

'That sounds reasonable enough.'

Christophe drank some beer and lay back

in his chair. He had taken off his jacket and had rolled his shirt sleeves up from the smooth brown forearms. 'Of course,' he said, 'the real reason why Charles hates me has nothing whatever to do with my activities. He would hate me if I did nothing at all.'

'Why is that?'

Christophe smiled. 'It is natural enough. He cannot bear to have a brother who is coloured.'

Radford spilled some beer. It made a dark stain on the right leg of his trousers. He stared at Christophe. 'You are Charles's brother?'

'More accurately, half-brother. We had the same father.'

Radford could see it clearly now — the resemblance to Lamartine. It was this of course that had made him think he had seen Christophe before. Now, looking at the man, he could see in those darkly handsome features the shadow of both Charles and Toni. This was why she had become so incensed even at the mention of Christophe's name; in the mulatto's veins was the same blood that ran in hers.

'In some ways,' Christophe said, 'St Marien is a West Indian exception. Racial tolerance has not advanced here as it has elsewhere. People with white skins are still at the top and

look down on all the others. These Lamartines are especially proud.'

'But the father — '

'Old Pierre? Oh, he was like a king. He
took just whatever roused his desires, but that
was not tolerance. He had the power that
goes with great wealth. In the end it didn't
help him. You have heard how he died?'

'I heard he was murdered.'

'And you were told the reason?'

'I was told the motive was political.'

Christophe gave a contemptuous laugh.
'Yes, I suppose they would be bound to say
that. Perhaps they've even managed to
persuade themselves that it is true. It is what
they would like to believe. But it is not the
truth. Would you like me to tell you exactly
what happened?'

Radford hesitated. Charles was, after all,
his friend, and he was staying in Charles's
house, accepting his hospitality. Would it be
loyal to listen to some possibly slanderous
tale about the dead father?

Yet why should Christophe wish to
slander Pierre Lamartine if, as he said, the
old man had been his father also? Besides,
what harm could there be in hearing both
sides of the matter and judging between
them?

'Yes,' he said, 'I should like to hear.'

Christophe took another drink of beer and put down the glass. He shook his head sadly. 'Poor Anton.'

'Anton?'

'Anton Giraud. He was the boy who killed old Pierre.'

'Boy? — I heard he was a man.'

'Do you call sixteen a man?'

'No more?'

'Not a year.'

'Yet he was old enough to commit a murder.'

'There was provocation. It was because of his sister, Lucille. She was maybe five years older than Anton. After the death of the parents she had brought him up. He idolized her. She was a lovely girl, I can tell you, and clever. She earned a living making dresses; she was good at it. Maybe everything would have been all right if old Pierre had not set eyes on her.

'Lucille was nineteen at that time. Pierre was sixty. But even at that age he had a way with women. He had the money of course, but it wasn't only that, I think. Anyway, he took Lucille.'

'How do you know this?'

Christophe looked surprised at the question. 'How do I know? Why, it was common knowledge. Anton used to go around burning

75

with fury. But what could he do against old Pierre?'

'Except kill him.'

'As you say. But it took a long time for him to reach that point. Not until Lucille's body was found in a swamp did he get to it. But you can imagine the effect of a tragedy like that on a boy of his age and temper. It must have driven him mad.'

'Did she kill herself?'

Christophe shrugged. 'Who knows? It's possible. Old Pierre had finished with her. She was going to have a child. But I knew Lucille and I don't believe she would have taken her own life, not for any reason. Of course it could have been an accident; but why should she have been near the swamp at all? It was on the Lamartine estate, but there was no reason for her to go that way. The estate is very large, as you know. So if she did not go there to commit suicide and if it was not an accident, what is left?'

Christophe picked up his glass and took another drink.

Radford asked slowly: 'You think she was murdered?'

Christophe put down the glass. 'There was some talk that she had been pestering old Pierre. It was said that she had gone to the house one evening when there was a dinner

76

party. Pierre had had difficulty in getting rid of her. He wouldn't like that sort of thing. He wouldn't want it to happen again.'

'So you think he had her removed?'

'I'm simply giving you the facts,' Christophe said. 'You must judge for yourself as to what really happened. Either way, the effect on young Anton was what might have been expected.

'And now, of course,' Christophe said, switching to a new line, 'we have this fellow Blond. What is he doing there?'

'Very little. He seems to be taking a holiday.'

'I find that rather strange.'

'Why?'

'Is he a friend of Charles Lamartine?'

'I don't think so. As far as I know, Charles had never seen him until the day he arrived.'

'And yet he invites him to stay in his house. Salesmen are not usually so hospitably received.'

'Perhaps they have a lot of business to transact.'

'Yes,' Christophe said. 'That is very probable. I really think that is very probable.'

The door opened. Radford expected to see Madame Christophe, but it was not Marie who came into the room; it was a girl of about twenty wearing a plain white linen dress held in at the waist by a scarlet belt of shiny plastic. She was a little over medium height with a beautifully shaped body and long, slender legs.

She had not, it seemed, been expecting to see a stranger in the room and was a little taken aback. She hesitated in the doorway, embarrassed, apparently undecided whether to come farther in or to retreat.

Radford stood up.

Christophe said offhandedly: 'My sister Yvonne.'

Radford said: 'To complete the introduction — I'm Guy Radford.'

The girl smiled. 'Of course. Georges told me you were coming. I had forgotten.'

She was not like Christophe, and yet there was something in her expression that told that they were brother and sister. In a certain indefinable way there was more Lamartine in her than Christophe. Perhaps the most surprising thing about her was the colour of her skin. Her hair was raven black but the skin had so little pigment in it that she could have passed for white. Her lips were full but not negroid and her eyes were large and curiously lustrous. The eyes held Radford, fascinated him, so that he found it difficult to draw away his gaze.

He realized suddenly that she must think

him rude, for he had certainly been staring at her. He made an awkward, jerking movement of the hand, indicating the chair he had just vacated.

'Won't you sit down?'

She did so with a natural ease and grace that no school could have taught.

'I should have told you,' Christophe said. 'Yvonne lives with us. She works at Government House.'

'As a secretary,' the girl said. 'I am not a political animal.'

'In St Marien,' Christophe said, 'we are all political animals. No one can stand aside.'

One thing had been puzzling Radford for some time — the fact that Christophe seemed an educated man. Knowing his origin, it might have been expected that he would have been like the labourers on the estates or the workers in the mine, but he was obviously far superior in intelligence and knowledge to them. The girl also spoke well and could have passed in any company. He wondered whether old Pierre had paid for the education of these natural children. From all he had heard of the man, it seemed unlikely.

It was Christophe who gave the explanation.

'Perhaps I should have told you. You may be wondering about it. Our mother is dead.

She was a teacher. She was really a very clever woman.'

Marie came into the room and announced that the supper was ready.

Christophe got up from his chair. 'Come. Let us go and eat.'

7

The Fort

'What kind of machinery does Blond sell?' Radford asked.

'Several kinds,' Lamartine said. 'Farming, mining. He is a freelance, you know, not tied to any one firm.'

'And does he also sell guns?'

Lamartine looked startled. It was early morning and he and Radford were having a pre-breakfast stroll through the grounds. It was perhaps the most pleasant time of the day — warm but not yet too hot for comfort.

'What makes you ask that?'

'I happened to see into his room last night and there was a dismantled rifle lying on his bed. He'd been cleaning it, I think.'

A momentary frown of annoyance passed across Lamartine's face. But he answered with scarcely perceptible hesitation: 'Yes, I believe he does sell sporting guns — as a sideline.'

'Quite a versatile man.'

'Monsieur Blond,' Lamartine said, 'has more accomplishments than you might imagine. Shall we go in to breakfast?'

Neither Toni nor Nicolette was present at the breakfast table. Sophie was already there and also Monsieur Blond.

'Good morning,' Blond said. 'If it is a good morning. I believe there is some trouble at the mine.'

Lamartine looked at him sharply. 'Who told you that?'

'I forget,' Blond said. 'Perhaps it was just a whisper in the air. That man Dessine, the one who wrecked the earth-shifter, he has been discharged, I believe.'

'And if he has?'

'I heard that there has been some murmuring among the workers.'

'The workers are always murmuring. One takes no notice of that kind of thing. It is of no importance.'

'Human beings are important,' Sophie observed in a low voice. 'When a man loses his job, how does he live? How does he provide for his family?'

'I have never enquired,' Lamartine said. 'It is none of my business.'

'Surely it is the business of all of us. These people are fellow human beings.'

'You speak about matters you do not understand. These people you call fellow human beings are not like us and are not to be judged by our standards. They are little better than animals.'

'Even animals have a right to be treated with humanity.'

'Humanity!' Lamartine was beginning to raise his voice, stung by this argument from one who was usually so quiet and passive. 'What do you know of humanity? What do you suppose would happen to hundreds of employees, to the whole economy of this island, if the mine were to close?'

'Why should it close?'

'It would have to close if it were no longer profitable to run it.' Lamartine was beating the table with his fist to emphasize his points. 'And if I allowed every incompetent worker to retain his post just because he had a wife and children there would soon be an end to profit. Did I persuade Dessine to marry? Did I force him to father a brood of hungry brats? No. Then why should I be expected to make myself responsible for their welfare? I am a man of business, not a philanthropist.'

He stopped speaking, drained his coffee cup and put the cup down. Sophie remained silent. She sat perfectly still, her lips pressed tightly together, her hands folded in her lap. To Radford it seemed that she was paler than ever. Her skin had a transparent look about it, so that it was almost possible to see the fine structure of bone lying just below the surface. Lamartine stared at her for a moment as if waiting for her to speak, but when it became apparent that she had no more to say he pushed his chair back from the table and stood up.

'If you will excuse me. I have a lot of work to do.' He walked to the door with a brisk, even military step and went out of the room.

Blond sighed deeply. 'So impetuous, so very impetuous. It is not the way these problems should be settled. One should move with caution; one should never act on impulse but only after long consideration. Do you not agree, madame?'

She turned her head towards him, as if drawn by the sound of his voice. 'Sometimes,' she said, 'the long-considered act can be far more destructive than the impulsive one.'

Blond smiled. 'That is true, I think, only when the considered act is from its inception specifically designed for the purpose of destruction.'

'That is what I meant.' She hesitated a moment. Then: 'What have you really heard about trouble at the mine?'

'Rumours, madame, nothing but rumours. There is probably no truth in them.'

'But that is not your honest opinion.'

Blond lifted his plump shoulders and let them fall again.

'My opinion is of no importance, madame, of no importance at all.'

★ ★ ★

Radford had decided to spend the morning taking photographs.

Some distance behind Lamartine's house there was a hill, the lower slopes of which were clothed with trees. Higher up the trees gave way to grass and outcrops of bare rock. It occurred to him that he might obtain some good views from the top, so with his camera slung over one shoulder he set out to climb the hill.

It was a longer climb than he had imagined and the summit was not quite what he expected. He saw now that it was not in fact a conical hill as he had supposed but a long ridge stretching away ahead of him. About mid-way along the ridge was a square stone building that looked as though it had at one time been a fort, but which had now fallen into decay.

His interest quickened by the sight of this ruin, he pressed forward more eagerly until he came under the walls of the fort. Trailing creepers had grown over the rough stone and from crevices sprang ferns and even brightly coloured flowers.

There appeared to be no opening in the wall facing him, so he turned to his left and walked round to the other side. Here he discovered a doorway some three feet from the ground and no more than five feet in height. There was no door but he could see some rusty hinges fixed in the stonework to which a few pieces of charred and blackened wood still adhered, and he concluded from this evidence that at some period in the history of the structure the door had been burned.

More curious now to see what the interior was like, he scrambled through the doorway and found himself in a narrow passage built inside the thickness of the wall. The passage led away to the right, and Radford, having made his way along this damp and rather gloomy corridor, found himself very shortly at the head of a flight of worn stone steps. He descended these steps and came out into daylight on the edge of a square of open ground. From the fact that this was at a lower level than the ground outside the walls he deduced that it must have been quarried out for the probable purpose of supplying the material for the building.

Some other erections had once stood

within the square, but these had long since fallen into ruins and had been grown over with scrub and creeper, so that even their outlines were now scarcely discernible.

Radford was gazing at these relics of St Marien's violent past when he heard a girl's voice calling to him.

'Guy! What are you doing here?'

For a moment he failed to locate the spot from which the voice had come; then he saw her; she was standing almost immediately above him on the battlements.

'How did you get up there?' he shouted.

She pointed. 'There's a stairway.'

He looked in the direction she had indicated and saw a flight of steps, half hidden by some bushes which had thrust their roots into fissures in the masonry and had grown twisted and stunted, as though crushed into that condition by the presence of the stone.

'I'll come up.'

The steps were worn and cracked but still solid. They were a good ten feet wide, the wall bounding them on one side, nothing on the other.

Toni was waiting at the top. She was dressed in a loose-waisted cotton shirt and the briefest of shorts. Her long golden legs looked smooth as honey.

She said, half accusatory: 'Did you follow me?'

'No. I had no idea you were here.'

She did not look altogether pleased by the answer. She turned away from him and walked to the parapet and gazed out through one of the embrasures. He could see the movement of her buttocks under the thin, stretched material of the shorts. Her hair touched the collar of the shirt like a breaking wave.

'Why did you come?'

He unlooped the camera from his shoulder and held it swinging in his hand. 'I thought about taking some photographs.'

'Yes,' she said flatly. 'There are some good views from here.'

He moved up beside her at the embrasure. 'No one told me there was a fort.'

'No? It's three hundred years old. When La Fontaine revolted the French troops made their last stand here. In the end the soldiers mutinied and killed their officers. Then they threw in their lot with Fontaine.'

She said all this in an expressionless voice, like a professional guide relating history. There was a sense of restraint between them.

'From here you can see the sea.'

He looked through the embrasure and saw the shimmering blue of the water with glints of silver where the sun caught the ripples. There was a ship apparently motionless, perhaps five miles off shore, a ribbon of smoke drifting from its funnel.

'Do you often come up here?' he said.

'Sometimes. When I wish to be alone.'

'Would you like me to go?'

'Do you want to go?'

'I haven't taken any photographs yet.'

'You'd better take them.'

'Yes,' he said, but he made no attempt to do so. The camera hung from the strap in his hand.

'From here the horizon is said to be forty kilometres away.'

'It seems probable.'

'From that other wall you can see Portneuf.'

'I imagine so.'

'Are you going to take any photographs?'

'I don't think so. I'm a very bad photographer.'

'Then why did you bring the camera?'

He lowered it to the stonework at his feet and let the strap fall on it. 'It's something one does, I suppose. It's one of the modern toys that everybody has to play with. Then they inflict the results on other people. Do you see the ship?'

She moved back to the embrasure and

looked out also. The space was narrow for two of them. He could feel the pressure of her body against his own and the sudden quickening of his pulse. As on the previous evening, the attraction was there, the animal attraction.

He did not move. She turned slowly and he could feel her breasts rubbing across his chest. He made a mental note that she was wearing only the shirt and shorts, nothing else. Even her feet were bare.

'Do you want to be alone?' he asked.

'I did.'

'But not any more?'

She began to laugh. He held her arms in his two hands. He stooped and kissed the hollow between her shoulder and her neck. He could feel her shaking with the laughter; it set up vibrations in her body that communicated themselves to his. He lifted his head and saw beyond her through the embrasure the bright shimmer of the sea. The ship seemed not to have moved, but there was no longer any smoke coming from the funnel.

'I wanted you to come,' she said. 'I told myself I didn't, but really I wanted you. There, I should not have admitted that, should I?'

Again he felt himself being enmeshed. There was a web being spun around him and he was not really struggling. His mind urged him to break free while it was still possible to do so, but his body refused to make the effort. The trap was too sweetly baited.

His right hand left her arm and moved up under the shirt. She laughed again, ending with a kind of gurgle. She had closed her eyes and her head was tilted back and her lips were parted.

8

Only the Beginning

'It's getting late,' she said. 'We ought to go back.'

Radford looked at his watch. 'You think they'll wonder where we are?'

'I'm not worrying,' she said.

'Hungry?'

'Yes.' She laughed. 'People in love aren't supposed to care about food. I must be unnatural.'

'Perhaps you're not really in love.'

'Then I have no businesss being here with you.' She rolled over on her side and looked into his eyes as if searching for the truth. 'You do love me too, don't you, Guy?'

'If I don't, I have no business here either,' he said.

It was dodging the question, avoiding a straight answer. But she accepted it as an avowal.

'I wonder whether Charles is home yet,' she said. 'I must tell Charles.'

'Tell him what?'

'About us, of course.'

He stared at her. 'Tell him?'

She laughed again and kissed him. 'Not about this. That we're going to be married.'

It was the net drawing tighter.

'Oh,' he said.

She drew away from him and sat up. 'You do want to marry me, don't you? You haven't just been — '

'Of course,' he said. 'Of course I do, Toni.'

He reached up and pulled her down to him. It might not be so bad. There were a lot worse things in life than being married to Toni Lamartine.

* * *

Lamartine arrived back at the house almost at the same time as they did. He was in a raging temper and it was obviously not the time to talk to him about anything so frivolous as an engagement.

'That swine Christophe. He should be put in jail. He should be hanged.' Lamartine was so incensed he could not keep still. He kept striding about the room and banging his clenched right fist into the palm of his left hand, as if this were a substitute for punching Christophe's head. 'This is the result of a weak government. Petra treats these devils as though they were human beings, but they are not; they are animals and they should be handled like animals — with a whip.'

He was in such a rage that at first it was impossible to gather from him what had happened. Gradually it came out in little spurts of information like the successive eruptions of a volcano.

It appeared that the trouble had started with the dismissal of Jean Dessine. Strangely enough, even after the interview with Lamartine at which Radford had been present, Baraud had still postponed getting rid of Dessine, and it was only after renewed pressure from Lamartine that he had reluctantly taken a step that was most certainly repugnant to him.

'Baraud,' Lamartine fumed. 'He is another weakling. I cannot understand why my father ever promoted him. Well, that will soon be altered. There are going to be a lot of changes very soon, I assure you. And then we shall see who is master.'

Again he had rushed off on to a side track, but he came back to the main issue. Christophe, it appeared, had no sooner heard of the dismissal of Jean Dessine and the reason for it than he had called the mine workers out on strike.

'The mine is at a standstill; machinery is lying idle. And even if the workers at the

Varne River plant don't also come out on strike they'll be forced to close down there too if there's no ore coming through to them. Every hour is costing us God knows how many thousands of fontaines. It's — it's criminal.'

'Is it a hundred per cent walkout?' Radford asked.

'Yes. They have had the audacity to post pickets at the mine. Even if anybody wanted to go to work they would be too intimidated.'

'Can't you get military help?' Toni said. 'In an emergency like this we should at least be able to rely on the army.'

The suggestion astonished Radford. 'But the men haven't done anything illegal. Surely they have a right to strike if they feel they have a grievance.'

'It's open sabotage. No one has the right to sabotage.'

'Of course it's sabotage,' Lamartine said. 'And communism is at the root of it. Christophe is just using the Dessine affair as a pretext. I have talked to the President over the telephone. I told him the situation and begged him to send troops to the mine. He refused. He refused point blank. That's the kind of man he is. 'Have patience', he said. 'Negotiate'. Negotiate with Christophe! A waste of time.'

'Have you tried?' Radford asked.

Lamartine came to a halt in his restless prowling. He stared hard at Radford. 'Ah, I forgot. You are his friend. You think that a little soft talk over a glass of beer would settle this matter. It would not. The only answer to this kind of thing is force. That is all these creatures understand.'

'Do you know what the terms are for a resumption of work?'

'Reinstatement of the man Dessine, no doubt,' the girl said.

'That and more besides.'

'More?'

'They demand a rise in pay of ten fontaines a week.'

'It would not be a high wage even then,' Radford said.

'A rise of fifty per cent! It would completely upset the economy of the mine. And how long would it be before the estate workers demanded the same? And the dock labourers, the truck drivers and everyone else. No, if we do not stand firm now there is no telling where this will end.'

'Suppose the workers stand firm too?'

'Hunger is a strong persuader,' Lamartine said. He walked to the window and stood with his back to the room. He seemed a little calmer. 'Perhaps after all this is not altogether a catastrophe. Now we will break the union once and for all. When we have cleared up this business we will put St Marien on the right road. There are a lot of changes coming; yes, a lot of changes.'

They all heard the car stop in front of the house and the slam of the door. A moment later Blond came in. He had the rather smug, self-satisfied expression of a person who has heard of another person's misfortune.

'So the miners have come out on strike.'

'You are well informed,' Lamartine said coldly. 'Who gave you the news?'

Blond shrugged. 'It is all over Portneuf. Such information travels quickly, monsieur.' He sat down and dabbed at his face with a handkerchief. 'In such heat I am not surprised that no one wishes to work.'

'The heat has nothing to do with it. It is a political manoeuvre.'

'Yes, assuredly. I was merely joking.'

'This matter does not happen to be a joke.'

Blond stuffed the handkerchief back in his pocket. His skin had a shiny look, as though it had been freshly polished. 'I fully understand, monsieur. The question that arises, however, is how this affects us.'

Lamartine glanced at Radford and his sister. He said rather hurriedly: 'We will discuss that later. Meanwhile, I have some telephone calls to make.'

He walked out of the room and closed the door behind him.

*   *   *

Half an hour later Valland and Porchaire arrived together. Radford was passing through the hall when they came in: Valland, dark, saturnine, heavy; tiny Porchaire with his mincing step.

Valland said: 'Ah, Monsieur Radford. Still enjoying your stay in St Marien, I hope.'

'Very much,' Radford said.

'Of course congenial company makes the time pass very pleasantly.' Valland's tone was light, but there was no friendliness in his eye.

At a guess Radford would have said that Valland was a jealous man, and he wondered whether Valland still supported the idea of engaging him to work at the mine or whether he had had second thoughts on that subject.

Porchaire said in his unnaturally deep voice: 'You have no doubt heard about the problem that has arisen.'

'I've heard that the miners have come out on strike.'

'The matter will of course very soon be settled. The prosperity of this small country

98

of ours rests rather heavily on the operation
of the mine. It cannot be allowed to remain
idle.'

'You have a plan of campaign?'

'We have come to discuss a course of
action with Monsieur Lamartine. No doubt
we shall arrive at some method of getting the
wheels turning again.'

At that moment Lamartine himself
appeared. He was accompanied by Blond,
and rather to Radford's surprise, the four of
them, after a brief handshake, went into
Lamartine's study and closed the door. For
what reason, Radford wondered, was it
considered desirable to have a machinery
salesman present at a discussion of the
mining strike?

Well, it was none of his business — not at
present. Whether eventually he might become
involved remained to be seen.

★　★　★

During dinner that evening Lamartine was
called to the telephone. He was away for
about five minutes. When he came back he
was biting his lip. He sat down and drank
some wine; his hand holding the glass shook a
little. No one said anything. Lamartine put
the glass down empty. When he spoke his

voice, like his hand, shook with suppressed fury.

'That was Christophe,' he said. 'He wished to inform me that he has called out the workers at the Varne River plant. He also informed me that if the board does not agree to his terms by tomorrow he will order the plantation hands to cease work.'

Blond gave a little sighing expiration of breath. 'And that would endanger the sugar crop.'

Lamartine ignored Blond. He seemed to be speaking rather to clarify the situation in his own mind than to enlighten his listeners.

He said: 'This, of course, is only the beginning. Christophe is not really interested in the reinstatement of Dessine or a rise in pay for the workers. He wants power, and by this means he hopes to get it. It will not be long before he calls out the dockers and all the rest of them.'

'A general strike?' Radford said. 'Surely he won't go to such lengths as that.'

'He will go to any lengths.'

'It would paralyze the island,' Blond said.

'No!' The plates rattled as Lamartine's fist struck the table. 'It will not be allowed to happen. We shall act too swiftly for this Christophe. The time has come for us to take matters into our own hands.'

9

No Answer

The knock was so light that Radford could not be certain whether he had heard it or had merely imagined it. It was an hour since he had gone to his room but he had not yet undressed. He had been reading and smoking. Perhaps he had been smoking too much; his mouth felt dry.

When the knock was repeated a little more loudly he knew that it had not been imagination. His immediate thought was that it must be Toni, and then he saw the door-knob turn and the door slowly open. A woman's hand appeared, an arm. He waited for her to come fully into the room, but he did not move.

'Guy! Are you there?'

He stiffened suddenly. It was not the voice he had been expecting. He got up and walked to the door.

'Sophie! What is it?'

She said hurriedly, a little breathlessly: 'Were you asleep? May I come in? I must talk to you. There is no one else.'

Radford hesitated. He wondered what Charles's reaction would be if he were to discover that his wife was paying such a late visit to the guest's bedroom.

She seemed to sense his reluctance. 'Please! It is urgent. Please, Guy.'

He did not hesitate any longer. He took her arm and drew her into the room.

'Shut the door,' she said. He did so.

'You are alone?'

'Yes, I am alone.'

'Of course.' Her hand sought his arm, moved upward. He could feel the touch of her fingers on his face. It was as though the sound of his voice had been insufficient to convince her fully that it was he and this were a necessary confirmation.

'What is it?' he asked again. 'What's troubling you?'

'They are going to assassinate the President,' she said.

For a moment it failed to register. He heard the words, heard them with absolute distinctness; but the meaning did not reach through to his brain, perhaps because the brain rejected so fantastic a statement. He just stood there looking at her stupidly, at the blind eyes and the delicately formed face with its fine bone structure and flawless skin.

She said again, as though fearing that he

had not heard her the first time: 'They are going to assassinate the President.'

This time it really got through. It was more than a collection of words dropped haphazardly. It had meaning, a deadly meaning.

'Who?' he said. 'Who are going to assassinate him?'

'The instigators are Charles and Valland and Porchaire. Others too perhaps. The instrument will be Blond.'

'Blond!'

'Are you surprised? Did you really think he was just a salesman?'

And of course when it came to it, he was not surprised. When he had seen the rifle with the telescopic sight he had guessed. Yet it had been so fantastic to associate a fat, middle-aged man like Blond with anything so violent that he had dismissed the idea from his mind. Blond, a hired assassin! It was not possible. And yet why should assassins not be as various as other murderers? What but the crime had there been in common between Dr Crippen and Charles Peace, between Palmer the Poisoner and Burke and Hare?

'How do you know about this?' he asked.

'Charles told me.'

'Told you?' It was scarcely believable. That Lamartine, who treated her with such contempt, should confide to her a matter of such importance as this seemed utterly out of character. Perhaps she had been mistaken; perhaps she had misconstrued something he had said.

She said quickly, as if sensing his doubt: 'He did not intend to tell me. It was blurted out in a fit of anger.'

'What exactly did he say?'

She did not answer for a moment. She looked very pale and he saw that she was shivering. It occurred to him that she might be about to faint. He fetched a chair and made her sit down. She was wearing a dressing-gown of quilted satin and her hair was swept back and tied at the nape of her neck with a single ribbon. It made her look younger, even more defenceless.

'He was cursing this man Christophe and saying that it was all because of him that things had got into such a state. I can't remember everything he said; he was talking to himself more than to me and it went on and on. Then suddenly, because I was saying nothing, he seemed to fly into a greater rage and shouted: 'Why don't you say something? Have you lost your speech as well as your sight'?'

'He could say that to you!'

'It doesn't matter. That is not the important point. When he said that I felt compelled to make some remark, so I suggested that perhaps it might be best to let President Petra settle the trouble. And then in a moment, as if without thinking, Charles cried: 'Petra will settle nothing. It is Blond who will settle Petra'. As soon as he had said that he seemed to regret it. He stopped speaking abruptly and all I could hear was his breathing, very rapid, like a man panting after violent exertions.'

'You are sure that is what he said? You couldn't have been mistaken?'

'I am sure. I asked him what he meant, and he laughed and said it had just been a joke and that I had better forget it and go to bed. He said he had some work to do, and then he went out of the room and I heard him go downstairs. I didn't know what to do. I was sure it was not a joke. He was not in the mood for joking. And if it was not a joke it could only mean one thing — that Monsieur Blond is here to kill the President.'

'Why did you decide to come to me?'

'Who else was there to go to? Toni? Nicolette? They would not do anything.'

'What do you expect me to do?'

'You must warn the President.' Her voice was urgent. 'Don't you understand? His life is in danger. This tragedy cannot be allowed to happen. He must be warned.'

'Even if it is so — '

'It is. It is. I am certain.'

'Well, granted that it is so, do you think he would believe me? Do you think I would even get to the President's ear? I should probably be dismissed as some kind of lunatic.'

'Then you mean to do nothing?' There was a trace of scorn in her voice.

Radford was stung by her tone. 'I didn't say I would do nothing. There could be another way.'

'What other way?'

'Christophe.'

She looked puzzled. 'I don't understand.'

'Christophe is interested in Blond. He asked me to let him know if I found out anything about him. Christophe has influence. A word from him would carry more weight than any of mine.'

'Yes,' she admitted. 'Yes, that could be so. But how do you intend to get in touch with him? Are you thinking of going to Portneuf?'

'No, I don't think that will be necessary. Christophe has a telephone. I saw it when I was at his house. I can ring him up.'

'You must not let Charles hear you.'

'I'll be careful. Don't worry.'

She got up from her chair. 'I had better go to my room now. If Charles should come back he might wonder where I am.'

Radford took her arm and guided her to the door. He peeped out into the corridor. It was deserted.

'All clear, Sophie.'

He stood aside to let her pass. Her hand touched his for a moment and then she was gone. He gave her time to reach her own room and then he went to the stairs and down into the hall.

The telephone was on a table at the far end. Radford had no idea what Christophe's number was and there was no directory on the table, but he supposed it would be possible to obtain the number from the operator.

The only light in the hall came from a single wall bracket, the others having been switched off, and he could hear no sound in the house. He lifted the receiver to his ear. There was a lot of crackling like the background noise in a faulty radio. He waited. He waited for what seemed a very long time, while the crackling rose and fell in volume and nothing else happened. There was no dial on the telephone; apparently the automatic system had not reached St Marien, or at least not this part of the island. He depressed the cradle with his finger and released it. The crackling stopped for a moment, then went on again. There was nothing else.

He glanced over his shoulder, uneasily aware that Lamartine might walk into the hall and ask him whom he was trying to get in touch with at that time of night. He wondered what answer he should give to such a question and could think of nothing plausible. The warmth of the day was still trapped inside the house and he could feel a thin film of sweat on his forehead. His pulse was beating with abnormal rapidity.

'Come on,' he muttered. 'Come on, can't you?'

The voice was scarcely audible above the background noise. He just caught the faint set phrase: 'Number, please?'

He said, speaking in a low, distinct voice: 'I don't know the number. The name is Christophe — Georges Christophe.' He added the address. 'Can you get me the number?'

The operator seemed to be having difficulty in hearing too. He had to repeat all this in a slightly louder voice. It seemed to him that everybody in the house must be able to hear him. The operator said she would try to get him the number and the line was silent except for the crackling.

He waited again. The sweat beaded on his forehead and he wiped it away with his finger. In the telephone he heard a click and then a bell ringing. It rang for some time.

'I am sorry. There is no answer.'

'Try again,' he said. 'Keep trying. It is important.' The bell went on ringing.

Suddenly it stopped. A faint voice, infinitely far away, said: 'Hello.'

'This is Guy Radford. Is that Monsieur Christophe's house?'

'Yes, Monsieur Radford. This is Yvonne Christophe speaking.'

He could imagine her having been roused from bed. He said: 'I'm sorry to disturb you at this hour. It's important that I speak to Georges. Is he there?'

'No. He has been out all day and has not yet come home.'

'Do you know where I can get in touch with him?'

'I am sorry. He could be almost anywhere.'

'Damn!'

'Monsieur?'

'Nothing. Would you give him a message? As soon as he comes back.'

'Of course.'

Radford hesitated. What message could he leave with the girl? 'Blond is going to assassinate the President!' She might think he

109

was mad. And suppose the operator were listening. What would she think? But did it matter what anyone thought? The important thing was to get the warning through.

The girl's voice came again. 'Are you there?'

'Yes,' he said, 'I'm here. Will you tell him — '

'One moment. I hear the door. I believe Georges has just come in. One moment — '

He heard a rattle as she put the telephone down on some hard surface. A door slammed. For a moment the crackling eased and he heard a murmur of voices. The telephone rattled again.

'Christophe speaking.'

'Well, thank God you came back. Now listen, Georges — '

He had heard no one come up behind him, but a hand reached past him and depressed the cradle, cutting the line.

'I don't think it will be necessary to talk to Christophe,' Lamartine said.

Radford put the telephone down. 'So you have been listening.'

'You should have remembered that there is an extension in my study. I happened to be there with Monsieur Blond.'

Radford saw behind Lamartine the bulky figure of the other man. Blond smiled.

'The telephone is a dangerous instrument,' he said.

'Not so dangerous as a high-precision rifle.' Blond shrugged.

Lamartine said: 'I see that my wife has been talking to you. It was very foolish of her. This is not a matter in which women should interefere. It is not their business.'

Radford could feel the hard edge of the table pressing against his thighs. He said: 'I should have supposed that the assassination of a President was everyone's business.'

'So you believe we intend to liquidate Petra?'

'Does murder sound less distasteful when you call it that?'

'Murder is a strong word, Guy; a very strong word.'

'Isn't it the right one?'

'In a case like this, no. One has to look at this affair from a different angle. Petra is a bar to the continued progress of this island. To remove him is the only logical way of ensuring the future of our industry.'

'Perhaps I'm not a logical man. It still looks like plain bloody murder to me.'

'And what do you propose to do about it?'

'I shall warn the President.'

He could hear Blond wheezing a little. Lamartine rubbed his chin; he had not shaved since morning and the stubble was visible like dark shading.

'That, of course, cannot be allowed to happen.'

'How will you prevent it?'

'I suppose you would not be prepared to give me your word that you will forget all this and take no further action?'

'No.'

Lamartine sighed. 'I was afraid not. You leave me then no alternative but forcible restraint.'

There was a brief silence. Radford saw that Blond, in a negligent, absent-minded sort of way, was holding a small automatic pistol in his right hand. He looked faintly apologetic about it, like a man forced into ill-mannered conduct much against his natural inclinations.

The sound of the telephone bell shattered the silence. Lamartine put out a hand and lifted the receiver. 'Yes?'

Radford could hear the crackling in the telephone and a man's voice speaking. He could not catch the words.

'I am sorry,' Lamartine said. 'Monsieur Radford has gone to bed. He is feeling a little unwell and I could not think of disturbing him. I will tell him you called.'

He replaced the receiver. 'That was

Christophe. He seemed to imagine that you wished to give him a message.' He shook his head sadly. 'Really, Guy, I don't think you should have gone behind my back like this. You are my friend and guest.'

'Am I still your friend?'

'I hope so. I truly hope so. When this unfortunate business has been cleared up I trust we shall be able to come to an amicable arrangement in that other matter.'

'If this business is cleared up in your way,' Radford said, 'we shall never come to an amicable arrangement. I wouldn't work for you or your friends on any terms.'

'Well, that is up to you. But now I think you had better go to your room.'

'And if I refuse?'

Lamartine's face hardened. His eyes were cold. 'You are not in a position to refuse.' His right hand made a small but unmistakable gesture towards Blond's gun. 'We are not playing games. There is too much at stake. You will go to your room.'

'Like hell I will,' Radford said.

As once before, Blond showed how swiftly he could move when he desired to do so. The gun, gripped in his right hand, swung in a short arc. It struck Radford on the side of the head and darkness came with it like a black curtain sliding across the light.

10

Night Encounter

He was lying on the bed and the room was dark. His head throbbed and there was pain behind the eyes, as if somebody had put sand on the eyeballs. It hurt him to move them.

At first he could not remember what had happened. He wondered why he should be lying there in shirt and trousers with shoes on his feet. And then it came to him, the recollection of Blond's arm swinging and the sudden blinding explosion in his head, the plunge into unconsciousness.

They must have dragged him up to his room and lifted him on to the bed and left him there. Unless Charles had called the servants for that task. Either way, it came to the same thing.

He tried to sit up and pain flickered through his head and neck. He lay back again and it felt as though the bed were revolving giddily. He waited for it to cease its gyrations, then repeated the attempt, more carefully this time, taking it by stages. When he found the carpet with his feet he stood up. He felt sick

114

and his legs were made of rubber. He fought the sickness and groped for the light switch.

For a moment or two he stood blinking in the sudden glare and the sand grated at the back of his eyes. He walked to the door on his rubber legs. He tried to open it. It was locked. The key was gone.

He was not surprised; it was what he had expected. Until Blond's mission was accomplished he would be Lamartine's prisoner. For the sake of his plans Lamartine could not afford until then to risk letting him go free. Nevertheless, even though he had expected the locked door, Radford could not avoid a sense of outrage, and with it an added determination to thwart Lamartine at all costs.

If he had previously had any lingering doubts concerning the truth of Sophie's story or the conclusions which she had drawn, these were banished now. The conduct of Lamartine and Blond would have been ample proof even if Lamartine had made any attempt at denial. And he had not done so; he had practically admitted that Petra's assassination had been planned.

The question was: when would it take place?

Radford turned this over in his mind. Blond had been on the island for as many days as he had. He had probably been preparing the ground; a professional such as he would not like to be hurried; he would want to take his own time. Now, however, because of the strike it was possible that Lamartine and the others in the conspiracy would force his hand, not being able to afford to wait much longer.

For, of course, it must be a conspiracy. There would not simply be the assassination of the President and nothing else. After that would come a seizure of power, perhaps the setting up of a new head of government. And where in all this did the armed forces stand? Almost certainly some of the officers would be ready to throw in their lot with the conspirators and might even now be waiting for the signal.

And that signal would be the assassination of President Petra.

Christophe must have suspected that something of the kind was afoot. That was why he had been so interested in Blond. Somehow it was essential to get to Christophe, to warn him. But how?

There was a marble wash-basin in a corner of the bedroom. Radford went to it and washed his face in lukewarm water from the tap. He felt better after that. The throbbing in his head eased a little; the rubber legs stiffened. He put a hand to his temple where Blond had struck him with the pistol. It was tender and swollen; the skin had been broken and it had bled slightly. The water had started the blood oozing again. He dabbed at it with a towel, thinking.

He thought of the window.

He hung up the towel and put on his jacket. He switched off the light and walked to the window. Weak moonlight rescued the night from complete darkness. Radford stepped out on to the balcony and saw that all the bedroom windows on this side of the house were dark. He leaned over the railing and could discern just below him a faint glow of light escaping through the curtains of Lamartine's study.

It was, he judged, some twelve feet or so to the ground. He climbed over the railing, lowered himself to the full extent of his arms and dropped. It was a soft landing and he did not think that Lamartine or whoever it was in the study would have heard him. Nevertheless, he crouched there for a few moments, listening intently. A low murmur of voices came from the study, but there was no indication of any alarm. He got to his feet and began to walk towards the outbuildings which served as a garage for the cars.

The sound of his feet on the drive sounded

desperately loud in his own ears even though he was taking great care to move silently. He glanced back over his shoulder, half expecting to see Lamartine and Blond running after him, but there was no one.

The garage was part of a long, low building that in the old days had been used for the accomodation of carriages and other horse-drawn vehicles. At one end were the stables, no longer used as such, since neither Lamartine nor his sister had any love for riding; at the other end was the part that had been converted to the housing of the cars.

The wide, hinged doors were closed and Radford groped his way to the catch. He had been afraid that there might be a padlock on the door and was relieved to find that there was not. Apparently thieves were not expected; perhaps it was too difficult to dispose of a stolen car in St Marien.

Radford lifted the heavy iron catch and began to pull open one half of the double-door. The hinges had not been recently oiled and they made a thin screeching like a cry of pain. When he had the door fully open he stopped again and listened, pulse hammering. There was no sign that anyone had heard him.

He went into the thick darkness inside the garage and could smell the heavy odour of oil and petrol and rubber. He had already decided to take whichever car happened to be nearest the door, and this turned out to be the Mercedes. He was happy enough about this, since Lamartine had let him try out the Mercedes on the way back from the mine and so he was familiar with the controls. There was only one possible snag. He opened the door and felt along the dashboard; then gave a sigh. The ignition key was there.

Everything so far had been in his favour. It had all been unbelievably simple. Now he had only to drive into Portneuf to Christophe's home and inform him of the plot; the rest would be up to him. Really, Charles had been incredibly careless; he should have realized that, even though the bedroom door was locked, the balcony offered an easy way of escape to any reasonably active man. For a moment Radford hesitated with his hand on the door of the Mercedes, wondering where the catch could be. Then he gave a shrug, got into the car and started the engine.

He did not switch on the headlights until he was clear of the house. There was only one further possible obstacle that he could think of — the big, wrought iron gates at the point where Lamartine's private road joined the public highway. In Radford's brief experience these gates had never been locked even late at night, but he could not be certain that they never were. It would be the devil if in the end he were to be baulked by this one last barrier.

The private road was perhaps a kilometre in length. He saw the gates ahead flanked by the two stone pillars on which they were hung. The headlights picked out the intricate tracery of the wrought iron.

The gates were shut.

He stopped the car and got out. Behind him the road under the trees was dark; there was no sign of any pursuit. Yet he felt sure that Charles must have heard him drive away and it might have been expected that he would immediately follow in one of the other vehicles. There was a Jeep as well as Toni's Ferrari. It was, of course, possible that he might still come; there would be bound to be some delay while he went to the garage and started the engine. Certainly it would be wise not to waste any time.

Radford walked to the gates. They were not locked. He swung them open and walked back to the car. He drove out between the pillars and on to the public road. He turned left and headed for Portneuf, driving fast but taking no risks. Still at the back of his mind was the feeling that something was wrong, that all this had gone too smoothly. It was as if Charles had wanted him to escape and had eased the way for him all along the line. Yet why should he have done that? It was ridiculous. Unless. Unless Charles knew that he would never get to Christophe's.

It was then that he saw the other car. It was a big convertible and it was slewed sideways across the road. At this particular point the road was at its narrowest. It had been carved out of the side of a hill; on the right was a sheer wall of rock and on the left was a drop of at least a hundred feet. The convertible was halted in such a position that it was impossible for another car to get past it at either end.

Radford brought the Mercedes to a stop.

There were four men standing beside the convertible. As if at a signal they walked towards the Mercedes. One of them came round to the driving seat.

He said: 'How pleasant to meet you again, Monsieur Radford. Charles told me on the telephone that we could expect you. I am so glad you did not keep us waiting too long.'

The voice sounded faintly amused, faintly mocking, faintly vindictive. It was the voice of Victor Valland.

11

New Quarters

The convertible ran sweetly, the engine purring. Radford sat in the back with Valland. There were two men in the front. The fourth man was driving the Mercedes.

Valland had a gun. He had shown it to Radford as a warning. The others had guns. Radford had no gun. He felt like a poor relation.

'Where are you taking me?' he asked.

'To a place where you will not be able to do any harm,' Valland said. 'But you will be quite comfortable, I assure you. We have no wish to do you any injury unless you should make it necessary. But perhaps I ought to warn you that the stakes are too high in this game to leave room for any weakness.'

'Charles told you, of course, what I found out.'

'And that you intended warning our revered President Petra through the medium of Georges Christophe. That, if I may say so, would have been an incredibly stupid thing to do.'

'I should have called it a humane thing.'

Valland made a gesture in the gloom. 'Let us not talk of humanity. On that subject everyone has his own ideas. Would you call it humanity to throw this country to the communists?'

'I'm not interested in politics, only in saving a man's life.'

'He is an old man. He could not expect to live much longer, whatever happened.'

'Then why not let him die in peace?'

'We cannot wait so long. The situation is one of extreme urgency. Monsieur Radford, you are not a fool. You have seen what happened in Cuba. We have no intention of allowing such a calamity as that to befall St Marien.'

'When you speak of St Marien you mean, of course, the landowners, the rich.'

Again in the darkness Valland made a gesture of impatience. 'I was told that you had been talking to Christophe. I did not think he would so quickly infect you with the virus.'

'What virus?'

'Communism.'

'You make it too easy for yourself,' Radford said. 'You give your opponents the label of communist and that excuses any measures you care to employ to stop them — even criminal measures — even murder.'

The car swung round a hairpin bend. It had been climbing steadily for the last half hour. It went on climbing.

'One doesn't call it murder to execute a man for treason,' Valland said.

'Has Petra committed treason?'

'Treason by omission, by weakness, yes.'

'It is always possible to find a pretext for what you wish to do.'

'We need no pretext for doing right.' Valland's voice had risen a little. His temper was beginning to fray. The man in the front, the one who was not driving, said in a low, growling voice: 'Why do you argue with him? There is no need to argue. We do what we have to.'

The car bumped over some roughness in the road. The beam of the headlights wavered ahead, picking out trees, rocks, ferns.

After a silence Valland suddenly asked: 'Do you imagine you are going to marry Antoinette Lamartine?'

'What do you think?'

'I think you should go home. St Marien is not for you.'

'You don't want me to work for the Compagnie Minérale then?'

'It no longer seems to me a good idea. I do not think you are the man for us. It was, of course, Charles who first suggested it. Charles had great faith in your ability.'

'Had?'

'Probably he too is beginning to change his mind. The man we employ must be one on whom we can rely to carry out the policy of the board.'

'You mean he has to be a tool in your hands?'

'You are free to put it that way if you wish.'

'I wonder,' Radford said, 'whether this is the true reason why you wish to get rid of me.'

He felt Valland turn. 'What do you mean by that?'

'Perhaps it would please you to be sure that I would see no more of Mademoiselle Lamartine.'

Valland made no answer for a few moments. Then he said: 'Of course. I should have realized what a great attraction there is for you here. What richer prize could there be for a penniless adventurer?'

'Do you mind explaining?'

Valland was sarcastic. 'Really, Monsieur, you must not try to feign ignorance. I am sure you are perfectly well aware that under the terms of Pierre's will Antoinette was left a very wealthy young woman in her own right.'

'I did not know.'

'I find that difficult to believe.'

Radford said in a sudden burst of anger: 'I don't care whether you believe it or not. I'm not interested in your opinion. And in this matter, as in any other, I shall make my own decision. I need no advice from you.'

There was a trace of iron in Valland's tone when he spoke again; the urbanity that usually characterized the man had for the moment slipped away, revealing the ruthlessness beneath. He said: 'It might be wiser, nevertheless, if you were to leave this part of the world as soon as possible. For some constitutions the climate can be most unhealthy.'

'Is that a threat?' Radford asked.

'It is advice,' Valland said.

They had been driving for about two hours when they came to the end of the journey. Radford was not sufficiently familiar with the island to have much idea of the route they had taken. He knew only that the road for the last mile or two had been very narrow and rugged. It did not appear to be one that was much used.

The car stopped. The Mercedes stopped behind it. 'Get out,' Valland said. 'We are here.'

Radford got out. Valland followed.

The headlights of the convertible were still

on. They revealed a long wooden bungalow with a verandah at the front. Behind the bungalow was a thick belt of trees. There was no sign of life.

Valland spoke to the man who sat beside the driver. 'Wake the servants, Thomas. I could drink some coffee.'

Thomas walked up the steps to the verandah and thumped on the door, shouting: 'Wake up! Wake up, you lazy devils.'

Valland explained to Radford: 'The bungalow belongs to our friend Porchaire. He comes up here when he wishes to relax. There is a lake close by. Excellent bathing and fishing. Not that Porchaire swims or fishes, but he likes to provide his guests with these amenities.'

'Do you think Monsieur Porchaire would be pleased to know that you're using his mountain retreat as a prison?'

'Please,' Valland said, 'don't call it that. There is no reason why you should not enjoy your stay here. And Porchaire knows all about it. He wishes you to regard yourself as his guest.'

'Perhaps he suggested the arrangement.'

Valland laughed. He had quite recovered his urbanity. 'To tell you the truth, he did.'

A light had appeared inside the bungalow. The door was opened by a white-haired

Negro. He was wearing trousers and a shirt. The shirt had not been buttoned and his feet were bare. He looked scared.

'Who is it? What do you want?'

Valland went up to the verandah. 'You know me, Guillaume.'

The Negro was holding an oil-lamp in his hand. He lifted it so that the light fell on Valland's face. 'M'sieu' Valland. I didn't expect — it's late — '

'Never mind,' Valland said. 'There was no time to warn you. You will have three guests for a few days. Monsieur Porchaire sends word that you are to provide them with every facility.'

The old Negro nodded. He looked confused, as though he had not completely shaken off the sleep from which he had been roused and did not fully understand what Valland was saying. He just stood in the doorway, holding the lamp and nodding until Valland lost patience.

'Don't stand there like an idiot. Let us in. Go and tell your wife to make some coffee. Move yourself.'

'Yes, yes. Of course, m'sieu', of course.' He led the way into the house and lighted another lamp in a large luxuriously furnished room with walls panelled in knotty wood and a Turkish carpet on the floor. Then he shuffled away and Radford could hear him calling his wife in a thin, quavering voice: 'Simone! Simone! We have guests. Make coffee.'

Valland lit a cigarette. He looked at Radford with a slightly mocking expression on his face. 'Guillaume and Simone will look after you while you're here. They are competent if a trifle senile. I shall leave Marcel and Thomas to keep you company.' He smiled. 'And also, of course, to ensure that you do not leave before we wish you to.'

Radford examined the two men who were to be his guards. Thomas was powerfully built, with a thick neck and black hair. There could have been some Negro blood in him. He looked bad-tempered and had a way of thrusting his head forward, as though aggression were his chief characteristic.

Marcel, the man who had driven the convertible, was very different. He was much younger, perhaps little more than twenty; he had lank, yellow hair, a thin, narrow face and no lobes to his ears. His mouth was small, somewhat feminine in appearance, and he had the long, slender fingers that are often supposed to indicate an artistic nature but usually indicate nothing more than the possession of long, slender fingers. His voice was very soft; one might have imagined it had not yet broken.

'I should perhaps warn you,' Valland said, 'that both Marcel and Thomas are prepared to shoot you rather than allow you to escape. I suggest, therefore, that you do nothing foolish.'

'It would, of course, grieve you deeply if I were to be killed.'

Marcel laughed suddenly. It was in a way a startling, even shocking, outburst. It was high-pitched and giggling, like the laughter of the mentally deranged.

Valland said sharply: 'Stop that!'

Marcel looked at Valland and the laughter died away in a curious gulp. There was something strange about Marcel's eyes; there seemed to be no depth to them; it was as though they had been flat disks reflecting only what was outside them and having no inner life of their own. They were very pale eyes.

Guillaume brought in a tray with coffee.

'You are all staying, m'sieu'?' He looked at Valland inquiringly.

'No,' Valland said. 'Only three. Tell Simone to prepare the rooms.'

'Yes, m'sieu'.'

Valland and the fourth man went away in Lamartine's Mercedes. They left the convertible standing in front of the bungalow. The fourth man had scarcely spoken. Radford had not even learnt his name.

'We shall let you know as soon as the crisis is over. Meanwhile, enjoy yourself.'

'Swimming and fishing?' Radford said.

'Just so. Swimming and fishing.'

12

Nothing to Lose

Guillaume's wife Simone was so fat she seemed to fill the doorway like a plug of putty squeezed into a knot-hole. She looked younger than her husband; there was no grey in her hair and her teeth were perfect.

She said: 'How long you mean to stay?'

'Maybe two days, maybe three, maybe more,' Thomas said. 'Are you worried?'

''Course I'm worried. You want to eat, don't you?'

'We're only normal,' Thomas said. 'We don't live on air.'

'Then somebody better get provisions.'

Thomas stared at her. 'You mean there's not enough food up here for a few days?'

'Not if you want good meals. Not with three extra. Guilaume and me, we live simple. When M'sieu' Porchaire make a party he send up provisions first. More help too.'

Thomas swore.

Marcel said: 'You'd better fetch some stores. You can take the convertible.'

Thomas swung round on him. He seemed

132

to be in a black humour, perhaps because of the lost sleep. 'Are you giving me orders?'

'No. Only suggesting.'

'Why don't you go for the stores?'

'If you want me to, I will. Makes no difference. Somebody's got to go.'

'I don't mind going,' Radford said.

Marcel sniggered. Thomas scowled. The woman looked placidly unconcerned.

Thomas said: 'All right. I'd better go.' He spoke to Simone. 'You give me a list. No, I'll take Guillaume with me. He can get the stuff.'

'How far is it?' Radford asked.

Simone began to answer, but Thomas cut in. 'None of your business.' He turned to the woman again. 'Go and make out a list. Tell Guillaume we're starting at once.'

'Yes, m'sieu'.'

* * *

They had listened to the early morning news bulletin from Radio Portneuf on a transistor portable. There was no report that the strike had spread further. Apparently Christophe had not yet carried out his threat to order the plantation workers to lay down their tools. President Petra had appealed to both sides in the dispute to exercise restraint and not to

133

aggravate the situation. He proposed to broadcast to the people that evening.

Thomas said: 'He is still alive, you see.'

Radford said nothing.

Thomas said: 'You should accept the situation, monsieur. You cannot help the President. You have tried and failed. And after all, it is not your business.'

'It is every man's business,' Radford said.

* * *

The convertible drove away down the rough, narrow road with Guillaume sitting, stiff and upright, beside Thomas. He looked like a man doing penance. A small dust cloud rose from the back wheels of the car and then it was gone.

The air was warm. There was no wind. The sun beat down on the white roof of the bungalow and was reflected in a glare that tortured the eyes.

Radford said to Marcel: 'I'm going for a swim.'

Marcel weighed the air with the palms of his hands. 'As you wish. I shall accompany you, of course.'

'Are you going in too?'

'I never swim,' Marcel said.

Simone found a pair of swimming trunks

for Radford. She said: 'You will be careful, m'sieu'. A man was drowned in the lake two years ago.'

'I'll be careful,' Radford said.

There was a footpath leading down to the lake. It snaked through the trees and squeezed between outcrops of rock; then suddenly came out on to a pebbly beach. The view was magnificent. The lake stretched away for at least a mile, and beyond it mountains soared into a blue haze. The lake was a pale green and the air shimmered above it in the sunlight.

'What is the name of it?' Radford asked.

Marcel sniggered. 'Porchaire. What else? Everything round here is Porchaire.' Whether he wished it or not, a note of envy had crept into his voice.

'And you do not own so much?'

'I? I own nothing. I am a servant.'

'Yet you act for the capitalists against the workers. Why?'

Marcel opened the front of his shirt and showed his bare, hairless chest. 'Look at the skin. Do you see any black?'

There was a wooden jetty wading out into the lake and on the right of the jetty a boathouse. Marcel opened the boathouse doors and revealed inside a launch, shining with varnish and brass and chromium plate.

Beyond it was a dinghy with an outboard motor clamped to the stern and tilted clear of the water.

'Playthings,' Marcel said. 'Playthings for the guests.'

Radford was surprised when he dived off the jetty to find how cold the water was. He swam out about fifty yards and then trod water and looked back. Marcel was sitting on the end of the jetty, his legs dangling. He had a gun in his hand. As Radford watched, he took aim and fired. Radford heard the report of the gun and the vicious slap and whine of the bullet as it ricochetted off the surface of the water. It could not have been more than a few inches from his head.

He shouted at Marcel. 'What the devil are you doing? Are you trying to kill me?'

He heard Marcel's sniggering laugh, and then another bullet flicked past, spraying water at his face. He jackknifed, went down into the clear water and swam submerged until his lungs were tortured. He came up nearer the jetty and heard the crack of the pistol again. He took a deep breath and went under a second time.

When he reached the jetty Marcel was calmly blowing on the muzzle of the automatic.

He said: 'You ought not to go so far. How am I to know you are not trying to escape?'

'You damned crazy idiot,' Radford said. 'How could I escape in nothing but a pair of swimming trunks?' He was so angry he could hardly control his voice. The anger sprang from the panic he had felt when the bullets had whined past. It was not pleasant to be shot at. It was not entirely a new experience. He had been shot at in Cyprus while doing his National Service. He had not liked it then and he did not like it now.

Marcel sniggered.

'You might have killed me.'

'Oh, no, I could not have done that,' Marcel said. 'I did not try to hit you.'

'You went close enough. Are you so sure of your aim?'

'But of course. See.' He took a scrap of paper from his pocket, rolled it into a tight ball and tossed it into the lake, where it floated on the still surface of the water. He raised the pistol, took careful aim and fired. The ball jumped. Marcel grinned, pleased with himself. 'I have had a lot of practice. I am not a novice at this game.'

Radford climbed out on to the jetty and dried himself with the towel he had brought. Marcel watched him. 'Aren't you going in again?'

'No,' said Radford. 'It wasn't as enjoyable as I'd hoped.'

'Things seldom are. It is life.'

On the way back to the bungalow Marcel asked: 'Do you wish to get away from here?'

'What do you think?' Radford said.

'I think it could be arranged.'

Radford glanced at him sharply. The silly grin that was so often on Marcel's face had gone; now he looked perfectly serious, a different man.

'Will you explain just what you mean?'

'I mean that I could help you to get away.'

'For money?'

'For nothing.'

'Why should you do that?'

Marcel kicked a stone from his path. He was wearing green suede shoes and yellow socks. His feet were unusually small for a man of his height.

He said: 'I have no desire to see the President assassinated. He is a good old man.'

'Then why don't you warn him?'

'I warn him! No, that is quite impossible. If I did that I should be in bad trouble. Don't you understand I am dependent on people like Porchaire and Valland and Lamartine?' He spoke with a kind of disgust. 'What would my life be worth if I were to upset their plans?'

Radford wondered whether Marcel was putting on an act; perhaps amusing himself at the expense of his prisoner as a cat amuses itself with a mouse. But the young man's expression gave no hint that what he was saying was anything but the absolute truth.

'So you are willing to let me go? Now? Before Thomas comes back?'

Marcel shook his head. 'Oh, no. It cannot be done that way.'

'Why not?'

'What excuse would I have? You must see my point of view. Besides, if you went now you would have to go on foot. It might not be easy. My way you will have the car.'

'What is your way?'

'It is perfectly simple. All the best plans are simple. Tonight it is my turn to guard you in your room. I shall conveniently go to sleep. You will get out through the window and take the car.'

'Won't you get into trouble for going to sleep?'

'Trouble, yes. But not so bad. Any man may fall asleep. It is not always possible to stay awake.'

'And the ignition key?'

'It will be in my pocket. You can take it while I am asleep. Before Thomas wakes up you can be away. You will be safe from pursuit because there is no other car. What can Thomas do? There is not even a telephone.'

Radford looked hard at Marcel, trying to detect a sign of deceit. There was none.

'You really mean this?'

Marcel's right hand fluttered in the air. 'Why should I say it if I didn't mean it? What advantage would there be to me in making this offer if it were not genuine? I have nothing to gain. And what have you to lose?'

For a moment as Marcel put this final question Radford thought a flicker came into his eyes; but it was gone before he could really catch it and there was nothing; perhaps had been nothing. The eyes were pale, flat, expressionless, dead.

'What have you got to lose?' Marcel repeated.

★ ★ ★

At midday they tuned in again to Radio Portneuf for the news bulletin and heard that the strike had spread to the estate workers. All over the island the cutting of sugar-cane had come to a halt and the mills were idle. From one estate a report of arson had come in; fields of sugar-cane were said to be on fire. The report was unconfirmed. There had been a riot in the small town of Civray and shops had been looted. In St Clair an American holiday-maker had been assaulted by a Negro and the police had had to break up a hostile crowd. President Petra was said to be conferring with his advisers at the Presidential Palace. Georges Christophe, the union secretary had issued a statement setting out the requirements for a return to work and threatening stronger measures if the employers refused to negotiate. A spokesman for the Compagnie Minérale de St Marien had said that the company would never yield to coercion. If the men returned to work any reasonable claim for a rise in pay would be carefully considered.

'And rejected,' Marcel said.

He switched off the set.

★   ★   ★

When Petra came on the air at nine o'clock he sounded old and very tired. He began by giving a brief outline of the situation, and while he spoke Radford could visualize in his mind's eye that small, lined, white-haired man whom he had seen riding away from the Palace in the white Rolls-Royce. The voice was gentle, a little sad; occasionally it almost failed and it was possible to hear faint sounds of the President sipping water, the rattle of

141

the glass being set down.

'Certain elements of the extreme left,' Petra said, 'will most certainly make use of this opportunity to attempt the complete disruption of our economy. Others, on the extreme right, will hope to take advantage of the unrest to seize power. For the country as a whole the success of either of these two groups could only be a disaster of the greatest magnitude. It cannot, it must not, be allowed to happen.'

They could hear him sipping water again.

Thomas said, 'He is senile. Why did they ever put him where he is?'

Petra continued speaking. His voice was a little stronger. He said: 'I have been urged to use the armed forces to break this strike. I have refused to take such a step. The Army should not be used as a political weapon. I have also been asked to bring pressure to bear on the employers. Pressure in this context can only mean one thing — threats. I do not wish to use threats.'

Again there was a pause.

'Threats!' Thomas said contemptuously. 'As if that old fool could threaten anyone.'

The radio crackled. Petra's voice came through the crackling.

'I appeal to all who have their country's interests at heart to remain calm in this difficult time. I appeal to you not to throw St Marien into a bitter struggle which can benefit no one but those who are actuated not by allegiance to the Republic but by their own selfish ambitions. I appeal to you to demonstrate to the world that we in this small island are capable of conducting our affairs in a civilized manner and that we no longer resort to violence to attain our ends.'

He ended abruptly. A snatch of tinny music came from the transistor set. It was the St Marien National Anthem. Thomas switched the set off.

'I am against violence myself,' Marcel said with a snigger.

Thomas scowled at him.

13

Moonlight

Radford could see the shadowy outline of Marcel in the chair by the window. He heard Marcel's voice, scarcely above a whisper.

'Are you awake, Monsieur?'

'Yes,' Radford said.

'It is perhaps time to go.'

Radford got out of bed and put on his shoes and jacket, moving silently to avoid waking Thomas in the adjoining room. He walked to where Marcel was sitting.

'The ignition key?'

'It is in my left hand pocket. You will take it from me.'

It was ridiculous, Radford thought, Marcel could easily have given him the key. This was just play-acting. However, if that was the way Marcel wanted it, that was the way it had to be.

'Very well.'

He groped in the pocket and could feel the warmth of Marcel's breath on his neck. He felt a certain repugnance; there was a strange rapidity about Marcel's breathing, as though he were excited. Radford wondered why. It was not Marcel who was escaping.

There was nothing in the pocket except the key attached to a leather tab. It seemed that Marcel either kept his pockets remarkably free from the usual odds and ends or that he had purposely cleared this one of all but the key.

Radford heard the whisper of Marcel's voice close to his ear. 'You can find it, monsieur?'

Radford pulled out the key and straightened up. With an instinctive movement he drew away from Marcel.

Marcel sniggered softly. 'I don't believe you still quite trust me, do you? You think I may be playing some trick. Don't worry yourself. There is no trick. You have the key; the car is outside and there is petrol in the tank. Go, monsieur, and the best of luck.'

'Thank you,' Radford said. Perhaps he had misjudged Marcel. The fact that he found something repellent in the man did not prove that he was not honest. If it came to the point, there were probably millions of perfectly honest people in the world who would have been equally repellent to him.

'Thank you,' he said again. 'I shall not forget this.'

'I believe you, monsieur,' Marcel said.

Radford stepped out through the window on to the verandah. In the moonlight he could see the convertible quite clearly. Moving very quietly, he crossed the few yards from the verandah to the car and got into the driving seat. He pressed the key into its socket and switched on the ignition. For a few moments he sat there, moving his hands over the controls to make himself familiar with them. The engine would need to start at once; if it did not Thomas might be wakened by the noise of the self-starter. He had to make certain that that did not happen.

He pressed the starter and the engine burst into life without hesitation. He put the gear into first and let in the clutch.

The car was pointing in the wrong direction and he had to go past the bungalow to turn and then come back.

He made the turn quickly and felt his hands sweating. When he passed the bungalow the second time he glanced out of the side window and was amazed to see Marcel standing on the verandah with the automatic in his hand. He heard the sharp crack of the gun and a bullet ricochetted off the windscreen and the glass went into a star pattern.

Radford ducked, jabbed his foot hard on the accelerator and clung to the wheel.

Suddenly it was all blindingly clear. He had been right to mistrust Marcel. Marcel was nothing but a pathological killer; all he wanted was an excuse to shoot his prisoner and this was the way he had planned to get the excuse.

Something that felt like a red-hot iron seared Radford's cheek. Later he was to realize that it had been a bullet, but for the moment this fact did not register. He was merely aware of the flicking pain and of the car swinging to one side out of control, of himself fighting to hold it and failing; and then the sudden, splintering crash and the numbing blow on the left shoulder as he was flung across the seat.

The car had come to halt, half wrapped round a tree, and he knew that he had to get out of it quickly or Marcel would be there to finish him off. He struggled back along the seat, opened the door, tumbled out, ducked and ran. He heard the crack of the pistol and the whine of a bullet, and then he was in under the trees. He was about a hundred yards from the bungalow; he stopped for a moment and glanced back and saw Marcel coming at a run, and behind Marcel was Thomas in pyjamas, a gun in his hand.

He turned and started running again.

Marcel was not far behind and Radford's

shoulder was still hurting him. He had no idea where he was going; his one object was to get as far away as possible from the men with the guns, and to achieve this purpose he plunged blindly on over the rough, stony ground between the trees.

And then suddenly he was out in the open and the ground fell away in front of him. He was too late to save himself; he stumbled forward and went rolling helplessly down the slope. The ground levelled and he was brought to a halt, half-dazed by the fall. He looked back and saw Marcel appear in the moonlight at the top of the slope. A red flame spurted from Marcel's hand and a bullet whined past. He heard the idiot laughter of the man and knew that Marcel was enjoying himself, enjoying this game that must inevitably end in a killing.

Radford was up the moment the gun fired. He ran, crouched low, zigzagging, and heard Marcel fire again, twice. He wondered how many more rounds were left in the automatic and whether Marcel had any spare ammunition in his pocket.

Then in the moonlight he saw the lake in front of him. He had come down to it quite by chance by a different route from that which they had taken in the morning, but it was the same broad expanse of water that bore Porchaire's name. He turned to the right and began to run along the shore, the pebbles crunching under his feet. A glance over his shoulder revealed Marcel sliding down the slope, but he had a good lead now; Marcel had lost ground when he had paused to take aim.

Just ahead of Radford a small promontory of slightly higher ground with some trees growing along the ridge pushed a barrier into the water. There was no way round it and he had no choice but to climb, his lungs bursting and his leg muscles knotting with the effort. When he reached the top he looked back again and saw Marcel running along the shore and, farther back, Thomas also. He plunged through the trees and down the other side of the ridge and saw the jetty and the boathouse not a hundred yards away.

With a last desperate effort he put on a spurt and reached the boathouse before Marcel appeared over the top of the ridge. Without hesitation he went inside and closed the door behind him.

Along one side of the building was a boarded catwalk to which the launch and the dinghy were made fast. There was a tarry, oily, weedy smell and a sudden scuttering sound and then a plop which he took to be a rat diving into the water. Light came into the boathouse from the far end, which was open to the lake, and also from a small window above the catwalk.

Radford walked to the window and looked out. He could see the jetty and the stretch of beach lying between it and the promontory. He saw first one figure appear in the moonlight and then another — Marcel and Thomas.

It occurred to him that he had been a fool to take refuge in the boathouse, since the two gunmen were sure to search it before moving on. It might have been wiser to cut back inland, but it was too late to think about that. He could only lie low and wait.

Marcel was still leading when he reached the jetty, but he stopped there and waited for Thomas to catch up. They were both only a few yards away from where Radford was standing and he could hear Thomas yelling angrily at Marcel.

'Fool! Idiot! Imbecile! How did you let him get away?'

Marcel answered sulkily. The exhilaration of the shooting and the chase seemed to have worn off and he was probably thinking about the consequences to himself. 'I fell asleep. He must have taken the ignition key from my pocket.'

Thomas was panting. He was wearing just

the pyjamas and a pair of shoes. He looked slightly ridiculous, but Radford did not feel like laughing.

'Idiot! And now because of your imbecility he has got clean away. How do we explain that, eh? And the smashed car?'

'I don't think he has got away,' Marcel said. 'He would not have had time.'

'Then where is he?'

'I think he is probably in there,' Marcel said. He indicated the boathouse with a gesture of the gun in his hand.

'He had better be,' Thomas said.

Radford heard them coming towards the boathouse. He moved away from the window, lowered himself into the water and pulled himself under the boarding. The water was only about four feet deep at that point but it felt ice cold. He moved a little farther along in order to get behind the shelter of the launch's side and he heard the door of the boathouse open. Feet padded on the boards above his head, and then it was Thomas's voice again. 'Well? Do you see him?'

'No,' Marcel said.

'Look in the motor boat.'

He heard the shuffle of feet again; then the launch rocked as Marcel stepped into it. There was the sound of water slapping against timber and then Marcel's voice. 'He is not in here.'

'Of course not. He would never be such a fool as to walk into a trap like this. He gave you the slip.'

'I don't think so. He was not so far ahead.'

'Then tell me where he is.'

There was a pause. Then Marcel said; 'Perhaps he is under those boards.'

'He could be,' Thomas admitted. 'But how do we see?'

'Wait. I think there is a lamp somewhere.'

Radford could hear Marcel moving about in the launch and the water was slapping noisily.

'Ah, here it is.'

Suddenly there was more light above him. He could see it shining through the boards over his head.

He heard Marcel say: 'Now we shall soon find out if he is there.'

The side of the launch nearest the catwalk dipped as Marcel moved over. Light splashed on the water. Radford ducked beneath the surface and thrust himself out under the keel of the boat. He could feel it scraping over his shoulders and then he came up on the other side and was able to breathe again.

He had been afraid that either Marcel or Thomas might have heard the sound of his movement, but apparently Marcel had already caused so much lapping of water by his search in the launch that this had covered any other sound. Now Radford could actually see Marcel hanging over the stern and directing the beam of his electric lamp under the catwalk.

Thomas's voice sounded impatient. 'Is he there?'

Marcel had turned sulky again. 'No, he is not.'

'I told you,' Thomas said. 'Come. We have wasted enough time at this fool's game. Bring the lamp. We may need it if we are going to catch that devil.'

Radford heard Marcel get to his feet. There was just a chance that he might shine the lamp over the outer side of the launch, so Radford again lowered himself under the water and moved back to his former refuge beneath the boards of the catwalk.

Marcel must have stepped out of the launch at the same time as he was going under it, for when the voice came again it was just above him.

'What was that?'

'What was what?'

'I heard something moving.'

'The boat — '

Thomas's words were cut short by the

crack of Marcel's automatic. A bullet lashed the water.

Thomas was angry. 'Why did you do that?'

'Something moved, I tell you.'

'A rat. Come. He's not here.'

Marcel's feet padded along the catwalk. The door slammed. The boathouse was silent.

Radford forced himself to wait five minutes before climbing out of the water. He was shivering with cold and the wound in his cheek was stinging, but he ignored it. He stepped into the launch and searched for the engine cover. When he had found it he lifted it and then looked about for a tool-box. There was one near the engine. He took a pair of pliers and cut the leads to the sparking-plugs. Having thus effectively immobilized the launch, he left it and turned his attention to the dinghy with the outboard motor at its stern.

There was just a painter securing the dinghy to one of the upright posts supporting the catwalk. Radford released the rope and stepped down into the boat. There was a pair of oars laid along the thwarts and the crutches were hanging from lanyards. He slipped the crutches into the crutch plates, pushed off, and manoeuvred the dinghy out through the open end of the boathouse. He put the oars in the crutches and began to pull away from the shore heading out towards the centre of the lake.

When he had put about a hundred yards between himself and the shore he started the outboard motor. The moon, which was nearly at the half, lay directly ahead, and he took his direction from this, steering down a silver path and leaving a flurry of churned-up water astern. He had reckoned that the lake was no more than a mile or so wide, but after a quarter of an hour he came to the conclusion that either his reckoning must have been amiss or the dinghy was not making the speed that it appeared to be. There was still no sign of the shore for which he was making.

Ten more minutes passed. Above the chatter of the engine he imagined he could hear another sound, a kind of muffled and continuous roar. It puzzled him and made him uneasy for the simple reason that it was there and could not be explained. A few more minutes and it had grown louder; it was no longer possible to think of dismissing it as a product of the imagination.

At the same time the moon disappeared. Radford thought for a moment that it must have been obscured by a cloud, but almost immediately he realized that the black shadow looming up ahead of him was no cloud but an immense wall of rock to which the moon had lured him and behind which it had then treacherously hidden itself.

He noticed now a certain turbulence in the water. The dinghy was jumping about as though it had suddenly come to life. Some spray came up over the bows and dashed itself in his face. It felt ice cold. It stung the gash in his cheek.

Almost in the same instant it became evident to him what the roaring sound was: it was the thunder of a waterfall. He could now see white flecks of foam directly ahead, and sensing the danger, he put the helm over to bring the dinghy round. It heeled over for a moment or two, and then as he centred the helm came back to an even keel. It was still in the turbulence, but now the fall was on the left and the dinghy was running on a course that was parallel to the line of the rocky wall.

Until this moment it had not occurred to Radford that this shore of the lake might be any different from the one he had left. He had expected a shelving beach of shingle on to which he could run the dinghy; but if the whole margin of the lake on this side should prove to be formed of sheer rock he was in a difficult situation indeed. To go back would be to put himself in the hands of Marcel and Thomas, and if he waited until dawn to reveal a way out he would again be in danger of recapture.

He decided to continue a little farther on his present course and then try to find a beach. The shore might not be all rock.

As the fall receded astern the water became calmer. Then the moon appeared on the left and he felt that it was time to make another attempt at a landing. He put the helm over. The dinghy started to come round, and as it did so there was a jarring shock that sent him forward on to his hands and knees. Almost immediately he felt water flooding in and knew that the dinghy was finished. It had struck some submerged obstruction, probably a spur of rock, and this had ripped out the bottom.

The motor was still going, but it was doing no more than drive the dinghy all the faster to its inevitable destruction. Radford struggled to his feet and cut the engine.

In the sudden stillness he could hear the muted rumble of the fall and nothing else but the gurgle of water rushing into the boat. He could feel it going down under his feet, going with frightening rapidity.

He glanced towards the shore. It was in shadow, but perhaps the darkness there was not quite so dense as it had been in the vicinity of the fall. In any case, he had no choice but to swim for it; the decision had been made for him.

The water was almost to his knees. He took off his jacket and let it fall, and in that same instant the dinghy slipped from under him as though its last remains of strength had ebbed away and it could no longer support his weight.

He began to swim with an easy stroke that would conserve his energy towards a goal that he could not even see. He could only make a guess at the distance, but he felt confident that he could make it. It could not be very far but the great question was what kind of shore it would be when he reached it. Well, he would know the answer to that question before he was much older. When it came it was the wrong answer. His stretched-out hand touched the sheer rock and there was nothing to grasp, only an almost vertical wall, so smooth and slippery that even an accomplished mountaineer might have been defeated by its implacable surface. He swam along it, searching for a handhold. There was nothing but the same relentless wall.

The irony of the situation was borne in upon him with bitter force; he had escaped death from Marcel's gun only to find it by drowning. Marcel had been robbed of his pleasure all to no purpose. It was funny when you came to think about it. It did not make him laugh.

For the first time he began to feel despair sapping his will. And with despair came increasing physical weakness. He felt as though he were swimming in a bath of mercury, so heavy and sluggish were his limbs; and struggle as he might, he seemed to make no progress.

Gradually his movements became weaker and weaker, until finally he was powerless to prevent his legs from sinking beneath him. He gave up all hope then and waited for the dark waters of the lake to close over his head.

Instead, his feet suddenly touched solid bottom and he was able to stand erect with his shoulders six inches above the surface. Two minutes later he had dragged himself clear and was lying on a strip of hard shingle.

14

A Journey

The sun was lifting the early morning mist when Radford heard the engine. He had slept soundly, and now he felt stiff and dirty. The gash in his cheek that had been cut by Marcel's bullet was caked with dried blood; it throbbed gently.

He was lying on a bed of ferns under some trees which had provided him with shelter for the night. From these trees he could see the low ridge which separated him from the lake, and which he had climbed the previous night before lying down to sleep. The sound of the engine had awakened him, and now he was alert to the possible danger that might be heralded by that sound. He got to his feet, walked to the base of the ridge and began to climb.

When he reached the top he could see the lake spread out below him, brilliantly blue and glassy smooth except where the fall dropped into it away to his right. The launch was about fifty yards from the shore. It was moving slowly and there were two men in it.

He concluded therefore that they had repaired the wiring and now were hunting for him.

He lay on his stomach and watched them. Marcel was steering and Thomas was looking towards the shore. Radford did not think they had seen him; they were probably searching for the dinghy. Perhaps when they failed to find it they would come to the conclusion that it had sunk and that he had been drowned.

Suddenly he noticed that Thomas was pointing. He touched Marcel on the shoulder and appeared to say something to him. Marcel brought the launch round in a wide curve and the engine note faded. The launch came to a stop, motionless on the placid surface of the lake. Thomas leaned over the side and pulled something out of the water. Radford saw what it was that had caught the man's attention. It was an oar.

Marcel had turned away from the wheel and he and Thomas were holding the oar between them. It was obvious that they were talking about it and no doubt discussing the implication of the discovery. Radford saw them put the oar down in the launch and gaze in the direction of the waterfall. It was not difficult to guess the thoughts that were working in their minds.

After a while the engine revved up again and the launch moved away.

It was thirst that plagued him most. His mouth felt like dried mud and his head ached. When he saw the house he judged by the sun that the afternoon must be well advanced. Since early morning he had been working his way southward, trying to get away from the mountainous region and eventually to reach Portneuf. It had been more difficult than he had expected; he was constantly coming up against natural barriers to his progress and having to make detours. Nowhere had he seen another living person or a sign that any other person existed.

Then in the afternoon he saw the house and the cultivated land below him. It was a long, single-storey, timber building with a verandah along the front, and it looked so much like Porchaire's bungalow that for a brief moment Radford wondered whether, after all his struggling, he had merely wandered back to the point from which he had started. A second look convinced him that this was not so.

Beyond the house the ground sloped down to fields of sugarcane, to plantations of banana and citrus trees. There was a prosperous look about the place, but it was strangely lifeless, as though it had been brought to this state of perfection and then had been suddenly abandoned.

There was a big shed with a red-painted corrugated-iron roof some distance from the house. A tractor and trailer were standing beside the shed. No one was using them.

A white road wound its way up from the lower ground to the house. There were grass verges on each side of the road. On one of the verges was a motor mower. No one was using that either.

There was a footpath leading down to the house and the outbuildings. Radford descended it with a vague sense of uneasiness troubling him. He could feel that there was something wrong here, though he did not know what it was. As he walked towards the bungalow there was a prickling sensation in his scalp. He was sweating and the palms of his hands were damp.

When he reached the verandah he saw the man. The man seemed to be asleep. He was lying with his face to the wall under one of the windows. Where he lay he was in the shade; it was probably cooler there.

Radford called to him, not loudly, somehow reluctant to break the strange, unnatural calm.

'Are you awake?'

The man did not move. He lay absolutely

still and there were flies crawling on him. Radford stepped up on to the verandah and saw the lacerations in the back of the man's head and the rents in his shirt. He saw the blood on the man and on his shirt, congealed like glue. He saw the blood trail leading to the door of the bungalow. He could hear the loud, obscene buzzing of the flies.

This man would never wake.

Radford walked to the door, treading softly, warily. The door was ajar. There was the mark of a man's hand on the door. The hand had been bloody.

Radford put one finger on the door and pushed gently. The door swung open soundlessly. He went inside. It was a kind of entrance hall with doors on each side and a passage beyond. The air was hot and still and heavy. Radford could feel the sweat trickling down his back.

There was blood on the floor of the hall, on the polished boards. A rug had been pushed up against the wall, perhaps in a struggle. The blood led to an open doorway. Radford followed it.

It had been a drawing-room. A woman's hand, a woman's taste were evident in the furnishing, in the vase of flowers, miraculously left untouched when so much had been over-turned, broken, destroyed.

The woman was there. Her dress had been ripped down the front, leaving her naked to the waist. She lay in a grotesquely unnatural attitude in a corner of the room, as though she had taken refuge there. The body had been mutilated and there were flies there too. Radford felt sick. He went out of the room and became aware of a curious moaning sound that seemed to be coming from the back of the house.

He felt the need for a weapon; at this moment he would have given much for Marcel's automatic. He had an urge to run from the house, out into the clean air, away from this polluted atmosphere, from this blood and horror. But he could not do that; he had to know the full story.

The moaning continued. He walked across the hall and down the passage.

He found them in the kitchen — an old man and an old woman — Negroes. The woman was sitting on a plain wooden chair rocking herself from side to side. It was she who had been moaning. The man, stooped like a bent nail, was standing with one hand on her shoulder, apparently trying to calm her. He stared when Radford walked in and the whites of his eyes showed.

Radford said: 'What happened here? Who killed those people?'

The woman broke into a storm of weeping. The old man moistened his lips. He stared at Radford with fear in his eyes. He said nothing.

'Did you kill them?' Radford demanded. He felt perfectly certain that these two had had no hand in the slaughter. There was no blood on them and they were too frightened. But he wanted to shock them into answering.

The man said quickly: 'No, no. It was not us. We did not do it.'

'Who, then?'

'The others.'

'What others?'

'The estate workers. They go mad. They kill with machetes. Then they run away.'

'Why did they do it?'

The old man made a little gesture of utter helplessness with his thin, veined hands. 'They hear about the strike. They come to M'sieu' Daumier and say to him: 'Give us more pay'. M'sieu' Daumier tell them they get no more pay from him. There is argument. They all get very angry. Start to shout. M'sieu' Daumier call them dirty apes. Then they go mad. They kill M'sieu' and Madame Daumier. Then they run away. Maybe go to Portneuf.'

'How long ago was this?'

'Two, three hours maybe.'

'And have you done nothing?'

Again the little helpless gesture of the hands. 'M'sieu', I don't know what to do. I am an old man — what can I do?'

Radford thought of the dead bodies, of the heat and the flies.

'They must be buried.'

The woman wept more loudly. The tears ran down her cheeks and trickled from her chin.

The old man said: 'I will fetch spades.'

It was late in the afternoon when they finished burying the bodies. Radford had set the woman to scrubbing away the blood. She had appeared reluctant to go near it, but he had ordered her to do it and finally she had obeyed. He could hear the sound of her scrubbing when he came in from the burial.

He felt filthy and contaminated. He found the bathroom and, peering at himself in a mirror, saw a haggard, unshaven face with dried blood and dirt adhering to it. He took off his clothes and showered himself with cold water. He found a razor and began to shave, avoiding the wound. It started to bleed again, but it was not deep and he was able to staunch the flow with some lint that was in the medicine chest.

He felt refreshed but hungry. He went to look for the old man and found him in the kitchen with his wife. She had finished scrubbing. Now she looked dazed.

Radford said: 'Can you get me some food? I haven't eaten since yesterday.'

The woman did not move. The old man spoke to her. She got up and began to prepare a meal. Neither of them had asked who Radford was or how he had come there. They seemed to accept his presence as a natural outcome of the slaughter. Perhaps they were glad to have someone giving orders; it relieved them of the need for independent thought or action. All their lives probably they had been told what to do, and without the guidance of a master felt helpless and afraid.

The woman served a good meal. She was calmer now, soothed by the execution of a task which she was used to doing. Radford ate in the kitchen, although this seemed to embarrass the two old servants. He was in no mood for ceremony.

He said: 'How far is it to Portneuf?'

It was the man who answered. 'Thirty-five kilometres, m'sieu'.'

'I must get there today. Is there a car?'

'The men took both cars.'

'All the same, I must get to Portneuf. You will have to come with me as a guide.'

The woman put a hand to her mouth. The

168

man said: 'I cannot leave my wife alone in this place. And it is too late to go today. It will soon be dark. Wait until tomorrow.'

'No. I must go today. Tomorrow may be to late. It may be too late even now.'

He could see in their faces that they did not understand what he was talking about. He felt it was useless to explain.

'You must come with me and show me the way.' The woman clung to the man's arm.

'No. Don't leave me alone. I am afraid.'

'There's nothing to be afraid of. No one will kill you.'

'I am afraid,' she repeated.

The old man said: 'You see, m'sieu'? It would be wrong for me to leave her. She is my wife. It would be wrong. Wait until tomorrow. Perhaps things will be different then.'

Radford saw that on this point he was not going to be moved. Whatever argument might be used to persuade him, he would stay with his wife.

'Then if you will not come you must tell me the way and I shall have to find it for myself.'

The man nodded. He seemed relieved that no more pressure was going to be put on him. 'Yes, I will do that. Certainly, m'sieu'. You will easily find the way. It is not difficult. You cannot go wrong.'

When they went out of the house the shadows had grown long. Radford saw the tractor standing by the shed.

'I'll take that,' he said.

The old Negro shrugged. He was passive. His master was dead and would have no more need of the tractor. Who was he to prevent a stranger from taking it?

'As you wish, m'sieu'.'

'Disconnect the trailer.'

'Yes, m'sieu'.'

Radford had had experience with tractors. He looked at this one and it presented no difficulty. It started easily. He put it into gear and drove off down the white road between the citrus trees. When he glanced back the old Negro was standing by the shed, motionless, watching. He looked like a man who had lost his way in life and no longer knew what to do.

★   ★   ★

Night came suddenly without the slow transition of twilight. Radford switched on the driving lights of the tractor and cursed its low speed. He had threaded his way along a succession of minor roads as the Negro had directed and had not yet found any sign of

170

the main highway to Portneuf. He began to wonder whether he ever would find it. Perhaps he should have forced the Negro to come with him.

The tractor died on him without warning.

He tried to re-start it. There was no response. Even before testing the fuel tank he had guessed the trouble. He was exasperated with himself for not having checked up before leaving the farm. Now the tractor was just a useless hunk of metal. It would never carry him to Portneuf or anywhere else.

He left it and went on on foot. The road was little better than a jungle trail. On each side trees formed a black wall and Radford no longer believed that this was the way to the main road. The Negro had said that he could not go wrong, but he had heard that tale before.

When the track petered out into a narrow footpath he debated in his mind whether to go back or not. But the idea of retracing his steps and passing again by the useless tractor did not appeal to him and he decided to press on in the hope that the path would lead him out on to another road or at least to some house where he could ask the way.

He was glad when he saw the light shining through the trees to his left. The moon had not yet risen and he could see scarcely anything of the ground that lay between him and that little yellow square gleaming out of the darkness. Nevertheless, reasoning that there could not be any impenetrable barrier between it and him, he stepped off the path and almost immediately found himself walking through knee-high vegetation which could have been grass. A short while later he was able to see that the light was coming from one of the upper windows of a house.

It was then that he noticed the scent of burning, or rather not so much of burning but of the charred wood and embers that are left after a recent fire. And in fact he could see a faint glow away to the right. The scent was very pungent.

When he came to the fence he was near enough to the house to make out the shadowy outline of its walls and roof in the starlight. The fence was about four feet high, three-barred. He climbed over it and heard a dog start to bark.

Almost immediately, as though he had only been waiting for this signal, a man appeared at the lighted window with a shotgun in his hands. He rested the gun on the sill and peered down at Radford.

'Stay where you are,' he shouted. 'Come a step nearer and I'll fill your carcase with lead. You hear that?'

'I hear it,' Radford answered. 'But I don't understand your reason. What have I done?'

'Who are you?' The man's voice was hoarse, as though he had done a lot of shouting already.

'My name is Radford.'

'What are you doing out there?'

'I've lost my way. I'm trying to get to Portneuf.'

The man appeared to consider this statement. Then he said: 'Are you white?'

'Yes, I'm white.'

'You don't sound like a nigger,' the man admitted. 'God knows what you do sound like, but not a nigger.'

'I'm English.'

The man was still suspicious. He said: 'Come into the light so I can see you.'

Radford walked towards the house. The gun pointed unwaveringly at him and he was only too well aware that just a small pressure of this man's trigger finger could send a cluster of leaden pellets tearing into his face and body.

He stopped in the light from the window and looked up. The light shone on the left side of the man's face, accentuating the profile. He had a nose like an eagle's beak, hooked and predatory, and his hair was grizzled. He was deeply tanned and could have been about sixty years old. He was wearing a check shirt, sleeves rolled up to the elbow. His forearms looked immensely strong.

He stared down at Radford for about ten seconds; then withdrew the gun. 'Yes, you're white. Alone?'

'Yes,' Radford said.

'Wait there. I'll come down.'

The man and the light disappeared from the window. After a few moments a door opened. Radford heard the man's hoarse voice.

'Are you there?'

He went forward. The man was standing in the doorway with the shotgun resting in the crook of his arm and an oil-lamp in the other hand. He was well over six feet tall, with powerful, slightly rounded shoulders. The dog, a big Alsatian, was at his side. It growled at Radford, but the man silenced it.

'Come inside — quickly.'

Radford went past him. The man closed the door and bolted it. He led the way into a room crammed with old dark furniture. He put the lamp on a table and Radford saw that the window was boarded up. It looked like recent work.

'Did you see any niggers roaming about?' the man asked.

Radford shook his head. 'It's too dark out there to see anything.'

'They burnt my outhouses down. They'd have burnt the house too if I hadn't driven them off with the gun.' He leaned it against the wall; it looked like a twelve-bore-double-barrelled. 'My name's La Scase. I winged some of the devils.'

'Why did they burn the outhouses?'

'They've gone mad. It's this strike. When the madness gets into them they just want to destroy, destroy.' He noticed the gash in Radford's cheek. 'You also have had trouble with them?'

'This?' Radford fingered the wound. It had dried again. It felt rough and brittle. 'No. A white man shot at me.'

'So?' La Scase looked hard at Radford. 'Whose side are you on, monsieur?

'I don't take sides. I told you. I'm English.'

'That is no reason. Where have you come from?'

'From the house of Monsieur Daumier. Perhaps you have heard of him?'

'Indeed. Yes. I know Daumier well.'

'He is dead. Also Madame Daumier.'

'Dead!' La Scase looked shocked. 'How did it happen?' Suddenly he seized Radford's arm in a fierce grip. 'That wound in the cheek. Was it Daumier? Did you — '

Radford twisted free. 'I did not kill Daumier. He and Madame Daumier were dead before I arrived. They had been murdered by their own workers.'

'My God!'

'When I arrived only two people were there — an old Negro and his wife who work in the house.'

'I know them,' La Scase said. He pushed his fingers through his grizzled hair until it was standing up straight all over his head. 'This is terrible, terrible. Poor Daumier. And Louise too. Such a fine woman.' A thought seemed to strike him. 'But what were you doing there? Was Daumier a friend of yours?'

'I never knew him. It was quite by chance I came upon the house.'

La Scase looked suspicious. 'It is not on the way to anywhere.'

'It would take too long to explain,' Radford said. 'The essential thing is that I get to Portneuf without delay.'

'I cannot help you. My car was in one of the out-buildings which those devils burnt down.'

'If you could put me on the way — '

'It is a long walk. At least twenty kilometres by road.'

'It will have to be done.'

176

'There is, however, a shorter way. The railway track from the mine passes near here. The railway takes a direct route where the road meanders. If I were to go with you as far as the track you could then follow it down into Portneuf. It does not go right into the town, but near enough.'

'I should be obliged if you would do that.'

The dog came with them. La Scase carried his shotgun.

'We may run into some of those black devils.'

'You dislike Negroes?' Radford said.

'Not when they keep their proper place. But when they think they are as good as we are, that is a different matter. Of course in the end they will take over this country. We are outnumbered. Sometimes I am glad that my wife and child did not live to see it. For myself, I no longer care greatly.'

'Is there any reason why black and white should not share the power? Why shouldn't they live as equals? Surely there is room for both.'

La Scase laughed harshly. 'That is a very naïve suggestion. It is obvious that you do not know St Marien. No, it has to be one or the other. If the white man once loses his grip, then he is lost completely. We shall be pushed under, trampled on. Those of us who are not slaughtered like poor Daumier will be forced into menial occupations. We shall be stevedores, bus drivers, cooks, labourers — '

'As the Negroes are now.'

'As the Negroes were intended to be.'

'By whom?'

'By God,' La Scase said.

They came to a post and wire fence. Beyond the fence Radford could see a gleam of metal.

'The railway,' La Scase said. 'You need have no fear of trains. Nothing is coming down from the mine.' Radford thanked him for his help. La Scase, with the gun in the crook of his arm, was a vague shadow in the starlight. He was not a likeable man; hard, bigoted, intolerant. Yet Radford could not help feeling a touch of pity for him in his loneliness.

'You did not tell me,' La Scase said, 'why it is so necessary for you to get to Portneuf tonight.'

'There is a plot to assassinate the President. I have to warn him.'

He could see La Scase's head lift. 'If I had known,' he said, 'I would not have helped you. It is Petra who has betrayed us. He deserves to be killed.'

Radford thought for a moment that La Scase was going to shoot him. He half raised

178

the gun; but then he turned and almost instantly was swallowed by the darkness. The dog went with him.

Radford climbed over the fence and on to the railway.

15

The Bridge

It was a single track. He walked on the sleepers, heading south. The sleepers were just a little too far apart for his normal pace; he had to stretch.

La Scase had told him that the distance to Portneuf by this route was some twelve kilometres. He reckoned that he should be able to make it in two hours without much difficulty. One thing at least was certain — he could not miss the way; there were no branch-lines.

He had been walking for nearly an hour when he noticed that it was becoming less dark. The moon was rising, and soon he was able to see some distance down the railway line. It stretched straight ahead without a bend, like a finger probing the night.

Radford was tired. He had had a long, hard day and little sleep the previous night. Moreover, the events of the past forty-eight hours had entailed the expenditure of more nervous energy than anything that had happened to him since the days when he had hunted terrorists in the Trodos Mountains.

He had just decided to take a few minutes rest before going on when he saw the lights. They were straight ahead of him, numbers of them moving about near ground level. Instead of resting he walked on more rapidly, and soon he was able to see that the lights were in fact lanterns carried by men, perhaps a dozen or more of them. He could hear them shouting to one another.

They sounded highly excited. He could not be certain, but he guessed that they were Negroes.

He stopped. Some instinct of self-preservation warned him against walking unannounced into this gang of men. He did not know what they were doing on the line at that time in the night, but whatever it was it was not likely to be something at which his presence would be welcome.

Nevertheless, he was curious to know what was going on; and in any case, if he was to reach Portneuf, he would have to go past the men. Therefore, he stepped off the track and slid down the embankment on which the line at that point was built. Then, crouched double, he once again moved cautiously towards the men with the lanterns. Soon he was able to hear, not only shouting and high-pitched laughter, but also the metallic clang of hammers.

He caught too the reflection of the moon on water, and then he saw that there was a river and a narrow steel bridge which carried the line from one bank to the other. Some of the men were on the bridge and others seemed to be working at the base of the piles which supported it.

One thing was certain now: since the men were on the bridge and since this was the only way across the river, he could not get past them without being seen. He would have to wait in the hope that they would eventually go away.

He heard a man shout: 'Jojo! Jojo!' And then there was a splash, as though someone had fallen into the water; and this was followed by a lot of laughter and more shouts of 'Jojo! Hey, Jojo!'

He crouched down in the long grass at the foot of the embankment and shivered, feeling the cool night air through his thin shirt. He heard more shouts, more splashing, more hammering, more laughter; and he guessed that the men had been drinking. Some of the lanterns were stationary, having been set down on the ground or on the parapet of the bridge; others wavered to and fro like signals warning non-existent trains of danger on the line.

Ten minutes passed. The moon went behind a cloud. A light breeze whispered down the embankment. A lantern fell from the parapet and was snuffed out in the water below. Radford remembered that he had seen this river on a map of St Marien. It joined the Varne near Portneuf. He could not remember its name.

A sound like the shuffle of feet on shingle made him look up. He saw, immense against the sky, a Negro standing on the embankment and staring down at him. In the Negro's right hand was a machete.

'You there! What you do down there, hey?' The thick voice was slurred, half drunken.

Radford stood up. 'I'm not doing anything.'

'You spy on us. White spy! I make sure you tell nothing.'

He came down the embankment with a rush. Radford did not wait for him. He cleared the fence and heard the swish of the machete. The wires twanged.

There was a ditch running beside the fence. He took a leap and cleared it, dived into undergrowth and felt the ground wet and soggy underfoot. It dragged at him.

The Negro was shouting. The machete slashed at branches, creepers, bushes, but in the marshy undergrowth it was as dark as a dungeon. Radford lay in a trough of mud, listening to the sounds of his pursuer floundering about and slashing here and there in a drunken fury. Once the machete passed within inches of his head, but soon the Negro must have come to the conclusion that it was a hopeless search, for Radford could hear him grumbling to himself as he climbed back over the fence and up the embankment.

Radford waited. The voices faded. There was no more hammering, no more laughter, no more shouting.

He came out of cover and could see no one on the bridge. He clambered over the fence and scrambled to the top of the embankment. He began to walk towards the bridge.

★　★　★

The night erupted in a red fire spouting upward from the ground. The blast threw him off the embankment like a dead leaf blown by the wind. He rolled over and over, and the fence stopped him. There was a ringing in his ears and his neck felt as if it had been clubbed. He heard something drop with a clang on to the steel rails and there was a series of splashes as debris fell into the water.

The fire had gone immediately; it had been as momentary as the explosion, bursting into startling life and dying on the instant. Now

184

the moon, reappearing from behind the cloud, was the only illumination.

Radford pulled himself up with the help of the fence and was surprised to find he could move all his limbs. He crawled up the embankment on hands and knees and walked towards the bridge.

It was no longer a bridge. It was a mass of tangled steel, of twisted rails and girders, sagging to meet the water which flowed past this new obstruction with a roar like that of a weir.

He examined the wreckage. From the embankment it sloped down towards the middle of the river; there it disappeared below the surface for a short distance, reappeared and climbed up to the other bank. Although there was now no flat track to walk on, it still looked possible for an active man to clamber along the material that remained above water. Which left only the problem of crossing the gap in the middle. And even there it might be that there was enough of the bridge only just submerged to provide a foothold. Perhaps, after all, there would be nothing worse to do than a little wading.

He started to edge his way along the twisted steelwork, and in half a minute had reached the point where the wreckage dipped below water. Here the river, impeded on each side, rushed through the gap at an alarming rate, and it was at once obvious that, even if the bridge did lie only just under the surface, there would be no possibility of wading across; the pressure would have swept him away in an instant.

Radford thought over the problem. He was clinging to a thin handrail which had apparently been part of the parapet, and this rail was the last piece of the wreckage to disappear under the stream. Peering across the gap, he could just make out what looked like the counterpart of this rail rising from the water on the other side. It occurred to him that if the submerged portion of the rail was unbroken he might with its help be able to drag himself across even though he would have to go under for a short distance.

Accordingly he took a firm hold on the rail and followed it down into the water. The river was rushing past him now with tremendous force, but still for a time he was able to progress hand over hand towards the other side. Then the rail suddenly ended and his right hand, searching blindly in the dark torrent, could find no continuation.

The need for air had now become too imperative to be longer denied. In one last effort he pushed off from the rail to which he had been clinging and kicked towards the opposite side. His fingers just touched some projecting spur of metal but could not grasp it, and in a moment he had been swept from the bridge and away downstream.

He came to the surface almost immediately and sucked air into his anguished lungs, not struggling, just letting himself be borne along by the current. He had hoped to avoid another swim, but it had come to it after all.

Beyond the obstruction of the wrecked bridge the force of the current gradually slackened. Radford struck out towards the bank, thinking uneasily of alligators and those small but voracious fish which, it was said, could take the flesh off a man in less than a minute. But the bank was not far distant and he reached it easily without feeling any kind of jaws fastening on his limbs.

He had by now, however, been carried some way downstream and he found that here was no solid ground but a kind of swampy jungle where the branches of trees and trailing vines drooped towards the water and massive roots crept upward from the slime. He pulled himself up on to one of these roots and heard something move in the darkness with a stealthy, slithering noise, such as might have been made by a length of rope being drawn through mud. There was a glimmer of phosphorescence like the dull glow of a sulky fire. Momentarily it was there; then it had gone. He shivered, not only because of the cold.

The next move was to get back to the railway, and the most likely way seemed to be along the bank, treacherous though this might be. With the river on his left he therefore began a slow and laborious progress upstream, floundering through mud and shallow water, impeded by trailing vines and creepers and plagued by myriads of biting insects.

Ten minutes later he had found the railway embankment.

16

Brief Appearance

Standing at the door of Christophe's house with his finger on the bell-push, Radford could hear the bell ringing inside. He let it ring for a while, then removed his finger and waited.

It was not yet daylight. It was, he judged, about five o'clock and Portneuf had only just begun to wake. Radford pressed the bell again. He heard footsteps approaching the door. It opened. Yvonne Christophe stood framed in the doorway. She was wearing a pale blue dressing-gown and the light in the hall behind her made a silhouette of her figure. Her hair was disordered, probably just as it had been when she had got out of bed to come down and open the door. She stared at him in amazement and then concern, but with immediate recognition.

'Guy! What has happened?'

He said: 'I'm sorry to come here at this hour and in this condition — ' He looked down at his muddy shirt and trousers — 'but it was necessary. I — '

'You must come in,' she said. 'You have been hurt — Tell me what happened. Your face — '

'Later,' he said. 'I must speak to Georges.'

'Georges is not here.'

'Not here? But — '

'He has been so busy — because of the strike. There is so much for him to do. He is sleeping at the union offices so that he can be on immediate call.'

'Then we can get through to him on the telephone?'

'Oh, yes. But what is it? Why do you have to speak to him?'

He hesitated for a moment, then decided to tell her. 'Georges asked me to find out why a man called Blond really came to St Marien. Blond is supposed to be a salesman. In fact he is a hired assassin.'

He paused. The girl did not speak. She waited for him to go on.

'He is going to assassinate President Petra.'

He heard the sharp intake of her breath. 'But why? Who would wish to kill him?'

'There is a group of men who believe that Petra is too weak. They want strong measures to be taken over labour questions. They want the union suppressed, and the first step towards that end is the removal of the President.'

She said: 'Is this true?' Then added quickly: 'But that is a stupid question. As if you would make up such a story.' Suddenly she appeared to remember something. 'This is why you rang the other evening and asked to speak to Georges.'

'Yes. I was prevented then from giving him the message.'

He saw that she understood. There was no need to elaborate. Nevertheless, one thing seemed to puzzle her.

'But why do you come to Georges?'

'Your brother has a position of influence. I think they would be more likely to listen to him than to me.'

She saw the point in this. 'I will try to get through to him.'

The telephone was on a table in the room in which Radford had talked to Christophe when he had first come to the house. Yvonne picked up the receiver. Radford watched her. Everything she did she did with natural grace, making the simplest movement into something of beauty. She had no time to attend to her appearance, yet it made no difference. Even like this, with the dressing-gown hastily thrown on and her hair disarranged, she was entirely lovely. She had no need of any artificial aid to enhance that loveliness; it, like the grace of her movements, was a thing of nature, hers by right.

He heard the click in the receiver as someone lifted the telephone at the other end.

The girl said: 'This is Yvonne Christophe. I wish to speak to my brother. It is urgent.'

Radford could not hear the answer, but he saw a slight frown on the girl's face.

She said: 'Yes, yes. I understand. Will you ask him to get in touch with me as soon as he comes in?'

She put the telephone down. 'He went out an hour ago. The man didn't know where he was going.'

'When will he be back?'

'He didn't know that either. Georges doesn't tell them everything, it seems.'

Radford looked at his hands. They were almost black with dirt. The fingers felt sore. His whole body ached. He said: 'I had better talk to the police. Do you know the number?'

She got it for him. The voice at the other end of the line sounded sleepy and bad-tempered.

Radford spoke slowly and distinctly. 'I wish to report a plot to assassinate President Petra.'

The man at the other end gave an exclamation. It sounded more of annoyance than surprise.

'Your name, monsieur?' There was weary resignation in the voice.

Radford said: 'My name is immaterial.'

'If you say so, monsieur. Perhaps you have more details?' It was possible to detect the irony even over the telephone. 'What method is the assassin going to employ — a bomb, a knife — poison perhaps?'

'He will shoot the President with a high-precision rifle.'

'Yes. It is a common method. A revolver pressed close to the chest is more certain; but the rifle — yes, it will do.' The man was mocking him, and Radford felt a wave of anger. He could feel the blood mounting to his face. 'And when, monsieur, is this deadly attack due to take place?'

'I don't know. Obviously it will be soon.'

'Oh, obviously. Perhaps you know where it will occur, even though you cannot state the exact time.'

'No, I don't know that either.'

'Oh, monsieur, how very annoying. It would have made the assassination so much easier to frustrate, wouldn't it? So what have we? Weapon — high-precision rifle. With telescopic sight?'

'Yes.'

'Of course. So we have one high-precision rifle with telescopic sight. Time — not known. Place — not known. That is correct?'

'What are you going to do about it?'

'Your report will be noted, monsieur.'

'Is that all'? Aren't you going to take any action?'

'Monsieur!' The voice hardened suddenly, losing all its mocking inflection. 'Do you know how many calls a day we receive from imbeciles telling us that the President is going to be assassinated? Dozens, monsieur, dozens. What would you have us do? Protect the President? We already do so. You may take it from me that where the President's life is concerned we take every precaution.'

'So you still refuse to do anything?'

'Your report will be noted.'

Radford heard the clatter of the telephone being hung up. The receiver was dead. He put it down.

'It's no use,' he said. 'They refuse to take any special action. They think I'm an imbecile.' He turned to the girl. 'I've got to get to the President. I've got to warn him. I'm not going to let Charles get away with this,'

She said: 'I think before you try to see the President you had better have a bath and a change of clothes.'

'But there's no time to waste.'

'President Petra is not dead yet,' the girl said, 'and I don't imagine your Monsieur

Blond is the kind of man who would break into the Palace and shoot him over the breakfast table. There is time for you to have a bath and some rest. Perhaps by then Georges will have come back.'

He saw the sense in what she said. If he tried to get into the Palace in his present condition he would almost certainly be arrested, and that would help no one.

'You are right,' he said. 'I certainly need a bath. And perhaps afterwards I might borrow some of Georges's clothing. We're about the same size.'

'I'll get some from Marie while you're bathing. She would soon be getting up anyway.'

Radford was apologetic. 'I'm being a lot of trouble. There's no reason why you should do all this for me.'

She smiled suddenly and he was dazzled. 'If it will make you feel any easier,' she said, 'perhaps we had better say I am doing it for the President.'

She was quite a girl, he thought; she was really quite a girl. He wondered how much of her character came from old Pierre and how much from the Negress schoolteacher who had been her mother. Perhaps in her the best of both had been subtly blended.

He awoke to the sound of her voice. He had been to sleep in one of the armchairs in Christophe's sitting-room, and he was wearing a pair of Christophe's trousers and one of Christophe's shirts. They were a little tight, but not enough to worry about.

It was broad daylight and Yvonne was speaking into the telephone. She was wearing a dress of gaily printed cotton that was drawn in at the waist and then flared out below the hips as though in the sudden joy of freedom. Her hair was in place and her legs and arms were bare, and she looked very cool and immaculate.

Radford heard her say: 'But I asked you to — Oh, well, yes, I suppose so. Yes, yes, please do that.'

She put the telephone down, turned and saw that he was awake.

'I rang up the union offices. Georges has been in, but they forgot to give him my message. Now he has left again.'

'And they don't know where he's gone?'

'So they say.' She came to the chair and looked down at him. 'How are you feeling?'

'Old and worn out.'

'You don't look either.'

'How do I look?'

She paused, as though considering the question seriously. Then she said: 'You look like somebody who has been in a battle.'

'I have, Yvonne; I have.'

She looked at him more closely. 'That — on your cheek — it is a bullet wound.'

He was surprised. 'How did you know?'

'I have seen many like it.'

'You?'

'When I was a child there was a revolution. It was suppressed. There were bodies in the streets after the soldiers had fired on the people.'

'I see.'

'In truth it was not a great revolution. A rabble of half-starved labourers demanding justice and receiving bullets instead. We had a strong president then, you understand. His name was Desmoulins. He was not like Petra.'

'And some would still prefer a Desmoulins.'

'Yes,' she said.

He asked suddenly: 'What time is it?'

'Ten o'clock.'

He jerked upright in the chair. 'As late as that! You should have woken me. I must go at once.'

'You mean to try and see the President?'

'Of course.'

'I think it would be best if I came with you.'

'But don't you have to go to work?'

'I am taking the day off. We shall have to walk, of course. The bus and tram drivers came out on strike yesterday.' She hesitated. 'That is if you don't mind being seen with me.'

'Why should I mind?'

'Some people might — '

'Yvonne,' he said. 'I don't care about people. I should be proud to be seen with you anywhere.'

He saw the rapid colour flood her cheeks. She seemed embarrassed. She said: 'I will ask Marie to make some coffee. It will not take a moment. You should have something before going out.'

She went out of the room.

* * *

Radford could sense an atmosphere of tension in Portneuf. It was as though the people were waiting for something to happen. They were like the dwellers at the base of a volcano that has started to rumble. There were not many private cars on the streets and the absence of trams and buses made it seem that the machinery of the town had run down.

But if the traffic was absent, people were not. Crowds of men and women wandered about, apparently without aim or purpose, or gathered in groups at street corners.

Many of the shops were closed and shuttered as if prepared for a siege; others seemed to be doing only a little business. Here and there a policeman, holstered pistol on hip and baton swinging, strolled with a kind of swagger, watchful, perhaps a little nervous behind the appearance of imperturbability.

'Whose side are the police on?' Radford asked.

The girl glanced at him. He could hear her heels clicking on the pavement. Without the constant grinding of motor traffic and the clanging of trams, other sounds were more noticeable.

She said: 'They should be neutral, shouldn't they?'

'Is anyone neutral in St Marien?'

She made no answer. They passed a soda-fountain with an enormous sign advertising Coca-Cola. It was perhaps an indication that the real key to the situation was not in St Marien itself but in the hands of American businessmen. Over all this part of the world lay the enormous shadow of Uncle Sam.

Voicing a thought, Radford said: 'I wonder whether it is ever possible for a country the size of this to be truly independent.'

Perhaps she too had noticed the Coca-Cola sign. 'You think we are tied to the dollar?'

'It usually comes down to a choice between that and communism.'

'Is there no middle of the road?'

It was a question he himself had asked Lamartine. There seemed to be no satisfactory answer.

'People who drive in the middle of the road often meet disaster.'

'President Petra is driving in the middle.'

'Yes,' Radford said. 'He is.'

★　★　★

The square in front of the President's Palace was crowded with people. They were pressed up against the iron railings and the gates that protected the forecourt. The sentries, prudently perhaps, had retreated to the inner side of these defences, and but for them the forecourt was deserted.

The crowd was remarkably quiet; there was little movement and only a low, continuous murmur of voices like the hum of innumer-able bees. Now and then, however, someone would raise a shout of 'Petra! Petra! Petra!', and this shout would gradually be taken up by more and more until the entire square was resounding to the cry of 'Petra! Petra!'

Radford looked questioningly at the girl. This was a quite unexpected obstacle.

'How do we get to the Palace now?'

'We shall have to push through the crowd.'

He stared at the packed mass of humanity and was dismayed by the prospect. 'Why are they here? What have they come for?'

'It is something that happens. Whenever there is any kind of trouble people flock into the square and shout for the President. Perhaps he will show himself on the balcony. He is very popular with the ordinary people. They feel they can trust him.'

They began to push through the crowd. There was no shade in the square and the sun was hot. Faces were gleaming with sweat and Radford could feel Christophe's shirt sticking damply to his back. He kept close to the girl. She still looked cool, apparently unaffected by the heat and the press.

At intervals as they edged slowly forward the shout of 'Petra! Petra!' would go up like a kind of chant. In a way it was frightening to be in the midst of it. There was here so much latent power, a great force that might get out of control, might sweep like a vast wave across the island, leaving destruction in its wake.

It took them nearly half an hour to reach the gates.

The gates were secured by massive iron bolts on the inside. Two sentries stood there, staring at the crowd with impassive faces. Radford called to the nearer of the two.

'I must speak to the President. At once.'

The sentry answered without turning his head, merely swivelling his eyes in Radford's direction: 'No one can speak to the President. You must write a letter.'

'You don't understand. This is a matter of great urgency.'

'All matters that concern the President are of extreme urgency.'

'Will you let me in?'

The sentry gave a short, coughing laugh. 'You — and all the others?'

Behind Radford the shout rose again. 'Petra! Petra! Petra!'

'They all want to speak to the President,' the sentry said.

The girl had been hunting in her handbag. She pulled out a small white card and held it up so that the sentry could see.

'Look,' she said. 'I am from Government

202

House. This is official business. We must see the President.'

The card seemed to throw the sentry into a state of indecision. It was probably, Radford thought, some kind of identity card issued to all those who were employed at Government House; but it had an official look about it and the sentry was impressed.

After a moment's hesitation he said: 'Wait here.' Then he did a smart right turn and marched off in the direction of what was probably the guardroom. A little later he came back accompanied by a sergeant. The sergeant was a stout man with a walnut skin, a black moustache and bulging eyes. His uniform looked as though it had been made for a smaller man, but it was possible that he had put on weight since it had been issued to him.

'Now,' he said, 'what is this all about, eh?'

The girl answered: 'We have to see the President on urgent official business.' She showed him the card.

'Let me look at that,' the sergeant said. He reached through the gate and took the card and examined it. He turned it over and looked at the other side which was entirely blank. Then he handed it back.

'This is very irregular,' he said. 'I shall have to ask the lieutenant about this.' He stared at the girl for perhaps twenty seconds with his shiny, bulbous eyes, turned as the sentry had done and walked away with a strutting, self-important step.

The sentry had reassumed his impassive expression. He said with a sideways swivel of the eyes: 'It's not usual, you see.'

Behind them came the shout again: 'Petra! Petra!' Then there was a sudden hush and a kind of mass gasp, as though everyone at the same time had said: 'Ah!'

'Look!' the girl said, pointing.

Radford saw a small figure come out on to the balcony at the front of the Palace. Even from where he was standing he could distinguish the white hair and the narrow outline of the face. Somehow, against the massive background of the building, the President looked even smaller and more fragile than he had looked when Radford had seen him in the car a few days earlier. He did not look like the kind of man who could successfully handle a political crisis.

He moved forward to the parapet at the edge of the balcony, rested one hand on the stone and raised the other above his head, as though blessing the crowd assembled in the great square below. One thought of a priest, perhaps a pope — a spiritual rather than a temporal leader.

Suddenly the people began to shout again in a kind of mounting frenzy: 'Petra! Petra! Petra!'

The thunder of their voices drowned all other sound. Even the sharp crack of a high-precision rifle could not make itself heard above that tumult.

Petra clutched at his chest, spun round and fell behind the parapet.

For a moment the crowd was stunned into silence, scarcely realizing what had happened. Then gradually, as understanding crept into the minds of the assembled people, a murmur began to make itself heard like the angry growling of a caged beast. It was the audible expression of rage and anguish and the sense of unimaginable loss.

Radford turned his back on the Palace and looked over the heads of the people towards the other side of the square. There was a row of tall houses over there with perhaps a hundred windows, from any one of which a marksman could have peered at a small, white-haired president through a telescopic sight. He would not be there any longer. Having squeezed the trigger, he would have melted away.

Radford felt the girl tugging at his arm and heard the urgency in her voice. 'We must go.

There's nothing we can do now.'

He had a sense of utter failure, of disgust with himself, of sick, empty bitterness.

'Nothing,' he said. 'Nothing. It has already been done.'

17

A Surprise for Lamartine

'I shall never be able to restrain them now,' Christophe said. 'After this killing there will be more and more. It will not end here.'

Radford had never seen him so angry. He could not keep still. He kept walking about the room, taking things up and putting them down again, as though astonished to find them in his hands.

'The fools! To do a thing like that! I should have seen it coming. I did see it. But I refused to believe it. I thought we had progressed beyond this kind of thing. Now I begin to wonder whether we shall ever progress.'

Christophe had been at home when they had got back. He had only just heard the news of the assassination. 'If only I had been here when you arrived last night. And yet, I wonder. Could I have done anything to prevent this tragedy? Could anybody? Perhaps it had to happen. But now — '

'You think there will be violence?' Radford said.

'There has already been violence. And it

grows like weeds after a rainstorm. Your friends are not going to stand still either, you know. No doubt they have their plans already made. What will you do now?'

'I shall go back to Lamartine's.'

Marie Christophe had washed and pressed Radford's clothes during his absence. She had also very neatly mended some tears in them. When Radford thanked her Christophe laughed.

He said: 'She knew I would want my clothes back. My wardrobe is not so extensive that I can spare any.'

Marie protested: 'It was not because of that. I would have done it anyway.'

'I am sure of it,' Radford said.

'How do you propose to get back to Lamartine's?' Christophe asked.

'Perhaps I can hire a taxi.'

'No. The drivers have joined the strike. There is no public transport of any kind.'

'Then it seems I shall have to walk.'

'It is a long way.' He thought for a moment; then said: 'I think the best plan would be for Yvonne to take you in my car. I have to go to the union offices, but we can go there first.'

'Won't you need the car?'

'Yvonne can bring it straight back. I can manage without it until then.'

'It's very good of you,' Radford said. He

glanced at the girl. 'You don't mind?'

'I shall be pleased to do it.'

The offices of the Amalgamated Workers' Union of St Marien were in a shabby building with peeling stucco walls in a narrow street near the waterfront.

A crowd of Negroes thronged the entrance, and when Christophe's Simca appeared they gathered round it so closely that Christophe had difficulty in opening the door. Everybody seemed to be talking at once, asking questions, shouting slogans, and all in a highly excited state.

'You see how it is,' Christophe said. 'People like this are not easy to control. They demand action. If you do not lead you are pushed aside and someone else takes over.'

Radford could appreciate his dilemma. Christophe might be honestly in favour of moderation, but when passions rose it was hopeless to preach that gospel. No one would listen. They wanted militancy, and if Christophe refused to be militant he would lose his grip on the union. In a way he was the prisoner of the very force which he had been largely instrumental in creating. He must lead it in the way it wished to go or he was finished.

'We are on a collision course,' he said. 'God knows what the outcome will be.'

He got out of the car and pushed his way through the crowd. Yvonne moved into the driving seat and the car slid away from the kerb.

'Poor Georges. He has worked so hard. And now — '

'You think he is bound to lose?'

'How does one fight against an army?'

'But the army isn't in the fight.'

'Listen to the radio at one o'clock and I am certain that you will find it is. Petra was not killed for nothing, you know.'

Radford saw that this girl had no illusions. She understood the way power was handled in a country like St Marien.

'You think that the union will be crushed and that the men will be forced to go back to work on the employers' terms?'

'Those who are still alive.'

'You take a very gloomy view of the situation. I'm sure Georges wouldn't entirely agree with you.'

'Hope comes naturally to Georges. Perhaps it clouds his judgement. I am a realist.'

Radford was silent. He glanced at the girl's profile as she drove. She was not only beautiful; she was capable and intelligent also. He had had proof of that. He could not avoid comparing her with Toni Lamartine, and in nearly every way the comparison favoured Yvonne. When they had left the town and were out in the country she asked suddenly, without turning her head: 'What are you thinking about?'

'About you.'

'I don't think I am a very interesting subject,' she said.

'On the contrary. And not only interesting but also very lovely.'

He saw her frown slightly. She said in a voice that vibrated a little: 'Just because you are alone with me you needn't feel obliged to talk like that.'

He was taken aback. 'You think it wasn't the truth?'

'I think it was an automatic reaction to what I said.'

'You certainly are a realist, aren't you?'

'I am sorry,' she said, 'but I have no taste for idle compliments.'

'No,' Radford said. 'I don't believe you have. Very well then; I think you're plain and unattractive and empty-headed. Does that satisfy you?'

For a moment he thought she was going to be angry. Then she began to laugh. 'I asked for that, didn't I?'

'I was speaking the truth the first time,' Radford said. 'I have no taste for idle compliments either.'

She glanced at him and then quickly back at the empty road ahead. 'I think,' she said in a low voice, 'that we had better talk of something else.'

'Why?'

'Because — ' She hesitated; then went on with a bitter vehemence that took him completely by surprise: 'Because you will soon be leaving St Marien and I am a half-breed.'

He stared at her. There was a fire burning in her cheeks and she seemed to be panting a little. Her words had come as a shock but as a revelation also. The implication did not strike him immediately. When it did he felt stunned and at the same time as though a great wave of delight were flowing over him.

Very softly he said: 'Yvonne!' And there was pleasure in speaking the name.

She would not look at him. She said: 'I should not have told you. I should have kept it to myself.'

'I am glad you didn't.'

'Why? Do you feel flattered to know that I could make such a fool of myself?'

'Why do you say that? Do only fools fall in love?' She did not answer.

'If so, I am a fool myself.'

She turned then. He could see the bright sparkle of tears in her eyes.

'You — ?'

'I think you had better stop the car before we have an accident,' he said.

★　★　★

She dropped him at the gateway to Lamartine's private road. She had been willing to take him to the door, but he had insisted on the other way in order to save her any possible embarrassment from an encounter with Charles or Toni. He felt that his own meeting with them might be difficult enough.

He kissed her hurriedly.

'Why did this have to happen?' she said. 'It can't work out.'

'It will,' he said. But he could see a lot of trouble ahead. It was impossible to blind himself to the fact that his wisest course would be never to see Yvonne Christophe again. Equally it was impossible to contemplate any such course. 'I love you, Yvonne,' he said. 'God help me, but I love you.'

He saw no one on the way up to the house. The door was open and he walked in. The hall was deserted. It was the first time he had been in the hall since he had tried to get through to Christophe on the telephone and had been knocked on the head for his pains.

He glanced at the telephone as if to draw some confirmation that the incident had really occurred. It seemed a long time ago, and yet three days had not elapsed in the interval.

The telephone was just as it had always been — a rather old-fashioned, spindly instrument. He was still looking at it when Lamartine walked into the hall.

Lamartine stopped dead when he saw Radford. He looked utterly amazed.

'You! But I thought — ' He swallowed audibly. 'I was told you were dead.'

'Perhaps I don't die as easily as some people. As presidents, for example.'

Lamartine did not respond to the remark. He said: 'I was told that you escaped in a boat and were drowned.'

'The first part of that information was correct, the second part false. Perhaps you would have liked it all to be true.'

'No,' Lamartine said. 'No, that is not so. When I heard of your death I was so angry I could have shot those two stupid fools on the spot.'

'Why didn't you?'

'They weren't here. They knew better than to come and tell me themselves. It was Victor who gave me the news.'

'Don't tell me that you shot him. I should

hate to think I had brought any harm to our dear Victor.'

'Now, Guy,' Lamartine said, 'don't talk like that. You must realize that everything we did was forced on us. Please understand that none of us had anything against you personally — '

'Oh, I am glad to hear that. It makes a knock on the head and a bullet wound in the cheek so much easier to accept when one knows they are presented without ill will.'

Lamartine came close to Radford and put a hand on his arm. 'I can understand your bitterness. But please believe me when I say that I would not have had this happen for the world. My instructions were that you were not on any account to be ill-treated.'

'It would not be ill-treatment, of course, to shoot me if I tried to escape.'

'I did not give those orders.'

'Valland did.'

'I gave him no authority.'

'Has it ever occurred to you that Valland makes his own authority, that he doesn't wait for orders from you or anyone else?'

He saw that he had touched on a sensitive spot. Lamartine drew his hand away and looked annoyed.

'However,' Radford said, 'your plans have worked out well enough so far. The President is dead.'

'So you have heard that?'

'I saw him shot. Monsieur Blond is an excellent marksman. Perhaps I ought to congratulate you on your choice of an assassin.'

Lamartine's face darkened. 'I advise you not to talk as freely as this in other company. You must understand that St Marien is not Britain.'

'You have told me that before. The fact is beginning to get through to me. I have had some rather intensive political instruction in the last few days.'

Lamartine took three or four paces down the hall, then came back. 'Don't you see that we have to take strong measures? If we weaken in the slightest there is no telling what may happen. These affairs have a way of getting out of hand in no time. Already people have been murdered, houses have been burnt, a railway bridge blown up.'

'I know. I helped to bury the Daumiers. I was at the bridge when it was destroyed.'

Lamartine was astounded. 'You were there?'

'I was walking back along the railway.'

'Then surely you realize how far these devils will go.'

'I realize that an old man has been shot in cold blood.'

'Very well, very well.' Lamartine sounded exasperated. 'So now what do you intend to do?'

'I don't know.'

'There is nothing you can do.'

He saw that Lamartine was right. Truly there was nothing he could do. He had had one small experience with the police and he saw little hope of their taking action if he went to them with his story about the authors of the assassination. In all probability he would simply find himself thrown into jail as an accomplice.

Lamartine went on in a conciliatory tone: 'I can understand your feelings. You feel outraged. But you must not judge what has happened here by the standards of, for example, a Western European country. We are not yet at that stage of development.'

'You are in the dark ages,' Radford said.

'Perhaps. Or shall we say with one foot in the past and one in the future? But, believe me, I should be very sorry if this were to affect in any way our friendship. I hope that, at least, will survive. I like you, Guy; I have always liked you, and I still hope that when you have had time to cool down and think things over you will decide to stay on in St Marien.'

'I don't think that is at all likely.'

'Well, we shall see. For the present anyway you will, of course, continue to be my guest.'

'You expect me to stay in the same house, to eat my meals with that murderer Blond?'

'Certainly not. We have finished with Blond. I never hope nor expect to see him again.'

It was what he might have expected. Blond, the instrument, the tool, had served his purpose and now would be cast aside, repudiated.

'I never cared much for that man,' Lamartine said.

18

Repercussions

There were four of them in the library — Lamartine, Radford, Nicolette and Sophie.

Radford had not yet seen Toni since his return. She had, it appeared, gone down into Portneuf. She must have got there before he and Yvonne had left, since they had met no red Ferrari on the road. He was not really looking forward to meeting her again; he felt that it could only be an extremely embarrassing encounter. He knew now that he could never marry her. From the first he had not been irresistibly drawn to the idea; he had been physically attracted, as any man must have been, but he had never felt any real love for the girl. It was she who had made the running and he had allowed himself to be drawn into an entanglement which, it had to be admitted, he had made only the feeblest of efforts to avoid.

Lamartine had told him that Toni had been very much upset by his disappearance. Apparently Lamartine had spun some story about a fishing trip with Valland to

Porchaire's lakeside bungalow. It must have seemed pretty thin; one did not normally set off without any warning on a fishing trip in the middle of the night. Besides which, Toni herself had said that Valland was no sportsman.

It was probable that Sophie had guessed the true reason for his disappearance, but no doubt she had seen the futility of taking any action and had kept her knowledge to herself. Toni had expressed her intention of going out to the bungalow herself, but Lamartine had persuaded her against this, and she had fallen into a sulky mood, keeping a good deal to her room and scarcely speaking to anyone.

★ ★ ★

There was a slight hissing sound coming from the radio in the library. Then a voice said: 'This is Radio Portneuf. Please stand by for an important announcement.'

Lamartine shifted in his chair. Sophie's hands were resting in her lap; she sat motionless and quite without expression. Nicolette looked sleepy; Radford wondered whether she had been drinking.

After a brief pause the announcer continued.

'As a consequence of the assassination of

220

President Petra and the rapid deterioration in the internal situation, it has been found necessary to proclaim a state of emergency throughout the island of St Marien. Until order has been restored and a new president elected General Madrin, Commander-in-Chief of the Armed Forces of the Republic has, with the assistance of the Defence Council, taken over the government of the island. Martial law is now in operation and all cases of insurrection or sabotage will be dealt with with the utmost severity.'

There followed a good deal more on this theme and then General Madrin was introduced. They could hear the General clearing his throat before beginning to speak in a harsh, rasping voice that seemed to blast the microphone.

'Fellow countrymen, it is with extreme reluctance that I take up the reins of government in this present emergency. I am not a politician. I am a soldier. I have no wish, and have never had any wish, to take part in any struggle for political power. Nevertheless, when law and order are being cast aside, when people are being murdered in their homes, when property is being destroyed and the safety of foreign visitors enjoying the hospitality of these shores is being threatened by unruly elements, then it becomes impossible to stand idly by.

'I am a patriot, and as a true patriot I cannot allow the good name of my country to be besmirched by the tools of an ideology that is completely alien to our national tradition. I call upon you all to obey the law, to return to work and not to compel me to take stronger action. I do not wish to use the power at my command, but I ask you to remember that it is at my command and that if necessary I shall not hesitate to use it. The choice is yours. I am confident that you will not choose wrongly.'

Lamartine switched off the set.

Nicolette said: 'Well, Charles, you always wanted a strong government. Are you satisfied?'

'This is merely a transition stage,' Lamartine said. 'That old fool Madrin is simply a weapon in our hands. When his purpose has been served he will go.'

'Perhaps you won't find him so easy to throw away as Blond,' Radford said. 'The taste of power may be too much to his liking in spite of what he says.'

Lamartine answered confidently: 'We can deal with Madrin.' He got up and went out of the room.

'Sometimes,' Nicolette said, 'I wonder which of my dear children I dislike the more.'

She too got up. 'It will not, of course, work out as Charles imagines it will. These affairs never do. We shall be lucky if it does not end with us all having our throats cut.'

'I don't think it will come to that,' Radford said. 'Not with the army in control.'

'But who controls the army? Madrin and his staff? Perhaps. But for how long?'

'You think there may be a mutiny?'

'I don't think anything. But I know that the rank and file are recruited from the very people who have come out on strike. They are from the same families. If the troops fire on the mob they may be firing on brothers, cousins, fathers. Do you think they will be happy to do that?'

'I don't know.'

'Neither do I. Neither does anyone. There is no way of predicting what will happen. For myself, I shall not even try.'

★ ★ ★

The camera was where he had left it. It was likely, he supposed, that no one had been to the fort since he and Toni had made love together. Unless she had visited it.

He walked to the embrasure and gazed out over the sea. He was surprised to see how dark it looked, as though some pigment had

223

been dropped into it and had impregnated the whole vast expanse of water. And then he noticed that there was a haze over the sun. The air felt humid and oppressive, making breathing difficult. There was no movement in it; everything seemed to have become hushed in anticipation of some great event, as the audience in a theatre is momentarily hushed at the rising of the curtain.

On the horizon a mountain appeared to have risen out of the sea, black and craggy and massive. It was still growing. Watching it, Radford saw a flicker of lightning streak across this sombre backcloth, and a little later he heard a low rumble like heavy artillery muttering in the distance.

Fascinated, he stood in the embrasure and watched the slow building up of the storm, watched the black shadow of nimbus creeping like death across the sky while the brilliant lightning danced along the horizon.

He felt a breath of air touch his cheek, and decided that it was time to go back to the house if he were to avoid being caught in the storm. He slung the camera over his shoulder and went down the worn steps from the battlements and out through the doorway in the wall.

The first big drops of rain were beginning to fall when he reached the house. He walked round to the front and was just in time to see a car driving away. In the car were Valland, Thomas and Marcel. It was accelerating rapidly. In a moment it was lost to sight round a bend in the road.

Radford went into the house and Lamartine met him in the hall.

'A terrible thing has happened,' Lamartine said. 'Really terrible.' There was a wild look in his eyes and all the blood seemed to have drained out of his face, leaving it a kind of muddy grey.

'What has happened?'

'It shows the lengths — it just shows — ' He took Radford's arm. 'Come into the study. We cannot talk here. My mother — Of course she will have to be told, but — it will be difficult but come, come.'

Radford allowed himslf to be drawn into the study. He had never known Charles so incoherent. He seemed to have had some kind of shock that had knocked him completely off balance.

Lamartine closed the door of the study. He said: 'They have killed Toni.'

It was Radford's turn to feel the shock. He could understand Lamartine's grey face.

'Who have killed her?'

Lamartine clenched his left first and gripped it in his right hand, as though

225

holding himself in check to prevent some uncontrollable act of passion.

'Those black devils, of course. They waylaid her on the road from Portneuf. Got her to stop by some trick no doubt. Dragged her into the undergrowth, stripped her naked and assaulted her. Then they killed and mutilated her.'

Radford felt sickened. He had never loved Toni, but he had had some affection for her. She had been spoilt by having too much money, too much of her own way, but she had never deserved this.

'Who found her?'

'Marcel Legrand. He was driving this way and saw the Ferrari standing by the side of the road. He recognized it and stopped to investigate. There was nothing he could do, so he went back to Portneuf, told the police and picked up Victor and Thomas.'

'Why did he do that?'

Lamartine shrugged. 'I didn't ask him. I suppose he knew the interest Victor had in Toni. Thomas happened to be with Victor.'

'Did Marcel see the men who did it?'

'No. They had gone before he got there. Not long though. The blood was fresh. He had some on his shoe.' Lamartine released the fist and banged it against his thigh. 'Those devils. Those black, murdering devils!'

Radford said quietly: 'How do you know they were black if Marcel didn't see them?'

Lamartine had walked a few paces away. Now he swung round and stared at Radford in utter amazement. 'Who else would have done a thing like this? Don't you see what it is? They are striking at me — me. In this way they insult me, taunt me. They throw this thing in my face. It is not enough that they murdered my father; now they must murder my sister also. And it is all to injure me, don't you understand? Me — Charles Lamartine.'

Radford was amazed now. Lamartine appeared to care less about the fact that his sister had been murdered than about the loss of face that he had suffered in consequence. It was the effrontery of the perpetrators of the crime that enraged him rather than the deed itself. Such egotism was scarcely credible.

'This is Christophe's work of course. He is behind it.'

'You have proof of that?'

'Proof! We don't need proof. We know. Well, we shall see how he likes the same treatment.'

Radford felt a chill in his spine as the import of Lamartine's words got through to him. 'You can't mean — '

Lamartine gave a sudden, savage grin that bared his teeth. 'I can mean. I do mean.

Victor is a very angry man. Have you forgotten that he was in love with Toni? You saw him drive away with the other two. If their destination is not Christophe's house I shall be extremely surprised.'

Radford thought of Yvonne, perhaps now back at the house. He gripped Lamartine's arm and shook him.

'You sent them there, you damned bastard! You bloody murderer! You sent them to Christophe's.' Lamartine was struggling to free himself. Radford let him go suddenly and he almost fell.

'I didn't send them. It was Victor's idea. Didn't you tell me he takes orders from no one?'

Radford forced himself to be calm. To beat up Lamartine as he felt like doing would not help Yvonne or Marie. Valland and the others had a good start, but it might just be possible to head them off. They might not go straight to Christophe's. It was the only hope.

He turned on Lamartine. 'Give me a gun.'

'What are you going to do?'

'Never mind what I'm going to do. Give me a gun, damn you.'

'What makes you think I have a gun?'

'Don't play with me, Charles. There isn't time.' Lamartine stared at him for a moment, then gave a shrug and went to a desk. He pulled a key from his pocket, unlocked a drawer and took out a revolver. It was a Smith and Wesson .38 with a four-inch barrel. He broke it open, put six rounds in the cylinder and handed it to Radford.

'You'll be a fool if you try conclusions with those three. Thomas and Marcel are professionals, and Victor is also a reasonably good marksman.'

'Don't let it worry you,' Radford said. 'And I'll take your car too, if you've no objection.'

Lamartine had become resigned. 'As you wish. I have to go to the police, but I can use the Jeep.'

'You're being sensible.'

Lamartine gave a twisted smile. 'That is more than I can say for you.'

★　★　★

When Radford left the house the rain was torrential and daylight had almost been blotted out. Zigzags of lightning lit up the sky and the rolling of thunder was practically a continuous sound. A gush of water pouring from the roof of the house overshot the gutters and fell in a wide cascade to the ground where it churned up earth and stones in a muddy conglomeration which rushed away from the walls towards the lower parts.

Before he had reached the garage Radford was soaked to the skin.

There were two vehicles in the garage — the Mercedes and the Jeep. Toni's Ferrari was missing, and Radford supposed that the police were keeping it for the present. Perhaps they thought they could learn something from it, or perhaps they just liked to hold on to red sports cars.

The Mercedes started at once and for the second time Radford drove it down the twisting private road and out between the iron gates. This time he did not imagine there would be any hold-up on the way to Portneuf; this time Valland and his associates were otherwise engaged.

The rain was like a single sheet of water spilling on to the car. The windscreen wipers were useless, and even with the lights on visibility was restricted to a few yards. Radford could feel the back wheels slide now and then on the treacherous road surface. He slowed momentarily, but then the thought of Yvonne Christophe goaded him and he let the speed build up again recklessly.

He had expected no hold-up, but there was one. On the outskirts of Portneuf a road-block had been set up, a white-painted wooden barrier.

Radford, driving fast in poor visibility, only

just managed to pull up without hitting it. The tyres squealed as he came to a halt within inches of the bar.

A policeman wearing a peaked cap and a black oilskin coat came round to the side of the car and tapped on the window. Radford lowered it.

'In a hurry, monsieur?'

'Yes,' Radford said. 'What is all this about?'

'A precaution, monsieur. Perhaps you have not heard. There is a state of emergency. You are going into Portneuf?'

'Yes.'

'On what business?'

'Why should I tell you that?'

'Because, monsieur, if you do not you may perhaps lose valuable time.'

'I am going to buy a hat.'

'Of course. Most urgent. Your name, monsieur?'

'Radford.'

'Nationality?'

'British.'

The policeman looked as though he found this in itself highly suspicious. The rain was streaming down his coat and some of it was being blown into the car. Radford was going mad with impatience.

'You are on holiday, monsieur?'

'Yes.'

'You have chosen an unfortunate time.'

'I didn't know the President was going to be shot.'

'This is your car?'

'No. It belongs to Monsieur Lamartine.'

The name seemed to have an immediate effect on the policeman. He said: 'One moment, monsieur. One moment.' Then he walked to a small hut at the side of the road and disappeared inside.

Radford waited. Time passed. He wondered whether to take a chance and try to crash through the barrier. He decided against it. The policeman came back with another man, apparently a superior. The second man poked his head into the car. He had a thick black moustache and discoloured teeth. His breath was like an attack of poison gas.

'You say that this car belongs to Monsieur Lamartine?'

'Yes.'

'Why are you driving it?'

'Because he lent it to me. I am his guest.'

The man with the moustache appeared to digest this information. Then he also said, 'One moment,' and walked back to the hut and went inside.

The rain fell without cessation. Minutes passed. Radford would gladly have shot the whole Portneuf police force. At last the man with the moustache returned.

'I have been in touch with Monsieur Lamartine by telephone,' he said, and paused, as though waiting for some acknowledgement of so remarkable an achievement.

Radford said nothing. The man with the moustache belched, bringing up an extra flood of poison gas. 'It is as you said, monsieur.' He sounded a shade regretful. 'All is in order. You may proceed.'

★ ★ ★

Portneuf was like a ghost town. The storm had driven everyone off the streets, and because of the strike there was scarcely any traffic moving. What there was seemed to consist chiefly of army lorries and Jeeps. In one square he saw a tank, motionless, the rain streaming off it, its gun depressed, in order no doubt to prevent water running down inside the barrel.

He took two wrong turnings on the way to Christophe's house. When he finally reached it the thunderstorm was still at its height and showed no signs of abating.

There was no car outside the house. Radford pulled in to the kerb, got out and walked up the short path to the front door. The door was open.

He pulled the gun out of his pocket and went inside. The body of the woman was in the sitting-room. It was lying face downward on the floor. They had shot her at least three times at close range. The woman's skin was black. It was Marie Christophe, not Yvonne.

The children were there too, the boy and the girl. Which of them had been killed first it was impossible to say. It made no difference. Death was the salient fact.

He put the gun back in his pocket and went quickly through the other rooms, calling softly: 'Yvonne.'

She was not in the house.

He went back to the sitting-room and stared at the dead bodies. It seemed strange that no one should have seen the men enter and leave the house, that no one should have heard the shots.

And yet not so strange. The storm would have covered everything. It had provided the perfect cloak for such business as this.

He left the house and closed the door behind him. He got into the car and drove to the offices of the Amalgamated Workers' Union.

Christophe was there.

19

Lebrun

He had never seen such anguish in a man's face. One by one Christophe touched the bodies, as though in the vain hope that in some magical way he might yet bring them back to life. Finally he stood up, looked at Radford and spoke one word.

'Who?'

Radford told him.

'Why?'

Radford told him that also.

The house was beginning to fill with people. There was a low hum of voices. Someone brought a sheet and covered the two children. Someone else covered the woman's body.

All the faces in the room were black. Radford could sense the animosity for him, the only white man. He felt that it would not take much to persuade these people to turn on him with their bare hands. There was no one else to strike at in revenge. He could easily become the scapegoat.

He said to Christophe: 'Is there anything I

can do?' Christophe looked at him as at a stranger. There was a wild, mad light in his eyes.

'No one can do anything for me. You had better go away before the fire burns you too.' His glance strayed to the sheets covering the huddled shapes on the floor. 'It is war now.' He stared again at Radford. 'Tell Lamartine — ' he said, and then stopped. 'No. Tell him nothing. Let him discover for himself.'

Radford hesitated. Christophe said suddenly, fiercely, 'Go now. Go, I tell you.'

It was a command not to be disobeyed. Radford turned and went out of the room. The people moved aside to let him pass, avoiding contact with him. They were silent, but even their silence he felt as an accusation.

They were gathering outside the house now. The storm had passed, but the darkness of evening had taken its place. The air smelled of the rain, and thousands of winged insects danced in the light of a nearby streetlamp.

As he was about to get into the car he saw Yvonne walking towards the house. She saw the crowd and hesitated for a moment before again moving forward. She did not notice him until she was level with him.

He said softly: 'Yvonne.'

She came to him quickly. 'Guy! Why are

you here? What are all these people doing?'

He wished that there had been some way of telling her without making it so brutal. But there was really only the one way. She had to know.

He opened the car door. 'Get in.'

She looked at him a moment, then did as he had told her. He went round to the other side and got in beside her.

He said: 'A terrible thing has happened.' And then he remembered that these were the exact words with which Lamartine had greeted him on his return to the house.

She said quickly: 'Georges has been killed?'

'No, not Georges. The others.'

'The — '

'Marie and the children.'

She seemed stunned. He went on talking. 'I tried to prevent it, but I was too late.' He reflected bitterly that it was his destiny to be too late. First Petra, now this. 'I came as fast as I could. There was a road-block. They held me up. But I don't suppose I should have been in time anyway. They had a start on me.'

She was staring at him. 'Who?'

'Valland and two others.'

'You knew they were going to kill Marie?'

'I didn't know for certain. I was afraid they — Toni has been murdered, you see.'

'Oh, God!' she said.

'Valland was in love with her. Charles told me they were coming here. I followed, but when I got here they had gone.'

'But I don't understand. Why kill Marie and the children?'

'Revenge. They blame Georges for everything. They have convinced themselves that he engineered Toni's death. This was to hit at him. No doubt they will try to kill him too. They may be looking for him now.'

'And he will want to kill them.'

'He said it was war. That is what it is.'

'I must go to him,' she said.

He watched her as she got out of the car and walked to the house. He watched until she had disappeared from sight and there was no more reason for staying. Then he started the engine and drove away.

★ ★ ★

Lamartine had left the house when Radford got back. He put the car in the garage and went up to his room. He took the revolver from his pocket and laid it on the dressing-table.

He went to the bathroom and had a shower in lukewarm water and changed into clean dry clothes. He picked up the revolver and put it in his jacket pocket. Then he went downstairs, just as Lamartine came into the house.

Lamartine was about to go into his study. He stopped in the doorway.

'So you're back, Guy. I am glad to see that you are still alive.'

'You have heard?'

'Heard what?' Lamartine sounded impatient.

'That your friends murdered a defenceless woman and two small children.'

Lamartine went into the study and switched the light on. Radford followed him.

Lamartine said: 'That really is a most hysterical way of putting it.'

'Is there anything hysterical about telling the truth?'

Lamartine walked to a cabinet and took out a decanter of whisky. 'Will you have a drink?'

'No, thank you.'

Lamartine poured a glass for himself and drank it neat. He said: 'More important things have happened than the deaths of three insignificant people.'

'The children were blood relations of yours.'

Radford saw Lamartine's face darken. 'Let us not go into that.'

'As you wish. What else has happened?'

'The garrison at Civray in the interior has mutinied and gone over to the side of the rebels.'

'I didn't know there were any rebels.'

'Call them strikers if you will. It seems they have got arms from somewhere. No doubt our communist friends could tell something about that. Already there have been clashes. Now this Civray garrison has shot half its officers and the others have joined the men. Madrin sent half a dozen fighter-bombers to attack the barracks and they shot down two with anti-aircraft fire. Madrin won't risk any more. The entire Air Force of St Marien only amounts to fifteen planes, now reduced to thirteen.' Radford could not help being grimly amused by the petulant way in which Lamartine related all this. He seemed to consider that it had all been done to spite him personally.

'So your wonderful schemes aren't working quite according to plan after all.'

Lamartine looked savage. He poured himself another whisky and drank it in one shot.

'You won't find it so amusing if these insurgents really get the upper hand. They may finish by killing all whites.'

'They wouldn't touch foreigners.'

Lamartine gave a harsh laugh. 'I don't

think I'd count on that if I were you. When they're fully wound up nothing stops them. Already an American has been knifed in St Clair.'

'That won't please the United States.'

There was the sound of a car pulling up outside, the slam of a door, then another, indicating that at least two people had got out. Lamartine had become alert, listening, his head tilted to one side. There was the faint sound of a bell ringing in the servants' quarters at the back of the house, then the shuffling step of one of the old retainers, a murmur of voices in the hall, more footsteps.

There was a knock on the study door; the door opened a little way and the manservant said: 'Monsieur Christophe to see you, monsieur.'

Christophe had not waited. He came into the study, dragging another man with him. The servant retired and closed the door.

The man with Christophe was a Negro. He was shabbily dressed and looked ill at ease. It was probably the first time he had been in such a house as Lamartine's. He was powerfully built and his hair was tinged with grey.

Lamartine said coldly: 'You have business with me?'

Radford had instinctively put his right

hand on the butt of the revolver in his pocket. He could imagine only one reason why Christophe should come to see Lamartine.

Christophe answered in a hard, controlled voice. He had, Radford noted, lost the mad look that had been in his eyes a short while earlier. Now the eyes were cold, the mouth set in an expression of bitterness. His movements, his speech, everything about him had a kind of deliberateness. He seemed to know just what he had to do and did not intend to allow anything to prevent his doing it.

'I have come to tell you who murdered your sister.' Lamartine gave a start. He glanced at the other man, as though he imagined that Christophe was presenting him as the guilty person.

'This man's name,' Christophe said, 'is Paul Lebrun. He is employed on the estate of Monsieur Daladier, which, as you know, borders the road between here and Portneuf. This morning he chanced to be near the road when something unusual occurred.'

'Why was he there? Isn't he on strike like all the others?'

'He was not working. He had gone to collect some tools that he had left.' Christophe turned to the labourer. 'Tell us what happened.'

The man cleared his throat nervously. His big, rough hands gripped the ragged trousers on each thigh, holding tightly to the faded blue cloth. His voice was curiously high-pitched, fluting. Coming from such a source it was incongruous.

He said rapidly: 'I see the car coming from Portneuf.'

'What kind of car?' Lamartine asked.

'A little, low, red car. There is a young woman driving. Then another car comes from the other direction — not fast — one man in it. The man makes some signal to the woman and both cars stop. The man get out and walk to the little car. He talk to the woman. I am behind a bush. They do not see me.'

'You are spying on them?' Lamartine said.

'I see them. That is all.' Lebrun sounded offended.

'Go on,' Christophe said. 'What happened then?'

'The woman get out of the car. She look one way and then another, maybe to see if anyone is near. Then she go into bushes on the other side of the road. The man follow — very close.'

'Did she go willingly?' Lamartine asked.

'I don't know.'

'Well, was this man forcing her? Twisting her arm or anything.'

'No, he is not twisting her arm.'

'Did he have a gun — a pistol?'

'That is possible. He have his back to me. It is possible he have a gun.'

'Go on,' Christophe said again.

'I wait. Ten — fifteen minutes later the man come out of the bushes. He look to see if anyone is on the road. There is no one. Some cars have passed, but they do not stop. Now there is no traffic. The man is in great hurry. He get in his car and drive off towards Portneuf. I think soon the woman come also, but she do not come. I go to look for her.'

'And you found her,' Lamartine said.

Lebrun nodded. 'I find her.'

'Why didn't you go at once to the police?'

'I am afraid, m'sieu'.'

'Why?'

Christophe broke in. 'Isn't it obvious? If he had gone to the police they would most probably have arrested him and charged him with the murder. They would have been only too pleased to catch somebody. So he came to me.'

'He took a long time about it.'

'I am afraid,' Lebrun said.

Lamartine sneered. 'And did you recognize this other man who so conveniently cropped up?'

'No, m'sieu'.'

'But you can describe him,' Christophe said. 'You can tell us what he looked like.'

'Yes. He is young. He have long, yellow hair and a thin face.'

'A white man, of course.' Lamartine spoke contemptuously. 'A likely story.' He turned to Christophe. 'You might have produced a more convincing tale than this. The fellow is obviously lying.'

'Why should he lie?'

'To cover up the real culprits. Your agents.'

Christophe took two steps forward and struck Lamartine on the mouth with the back of his hand. Lamartine staggered from the force of the blow and clutched at a chair to save himself from falling.

'Do not accuse me of such a filthy crime,' Christophe said. 'I am not the one who murders women and children.'

Lamartine stood with his back to the chair and an expression of venom on his face. He took a handkerchief from his pocket and dabbed at his lip. The handkerchief came away stained with blood.

★ ★ ★

None of them had heard the other men come into the house. The door opened and Valland came in. Marcel followed him and closed the

245

door. They seemed to have dropped Thomas.

Valland looked at Christophe. 'Ah,' he said. 'I was told that we should find you here.'

Lebrun had turned and was staring at Marcel. Suddenly he pointed a long, quivering finger and began to shout in his high-pitched voice: 'That is the man! That is the man!'

Radford saw Christophe move swiftly like a panther to bring himself into a position facing Valland and Marcel and Lamartine. In his right hand a heavy black automatic had appeared.

'Let no man move a hand,' Christophe said. 'Just keep them where they are.'

Valland said with studied insolence: 'You keep bad company, Charles.' He looked at Lebrun with fastidious disdain. 'Who is this creature?'

He ignored Christophe.

'He has come here,' Lamartine said, 'with some improbable story concerning the murder of my sister. He says it was done by a man with yellow hair.'

'That man,' Lebrun said. He pointed again at Marcel. 'I would know him anywhere.'

Radford looked at Marcel. Valland was looking at him also. Everyone was looking at him.

Marcel laughed nervously. 'What nonsense

is this? It was I who found the body. I informed the police. Would I have done that if I had killed her?'

It was Valland who answered — softly, musingly. 'Perhaps.'

'But why should I kill her?' Marcel stammered. 'What reason would I have?'

'Precisely,' Lamartine said. 'What reason would he have, Victor?'

'I can give you a reason,' Radford said.

He saw Lamartine's and Valland's heads turn to him.

'I think Marcel killed Toni for the same reason that he tried to kill me.'

Marcel spluttered. 'That is ridiculous. I shot at you because you were escaping. I was simply carrying out Monsieur Valland's orders.'

'After first helping me to escape.'

'What did you say?' Valland demanded.

'He told me that he was against the killing of President Petra and that he was willing to let me get away, and then he would give the excuse that he fell asleep.'

'It's a lie, a lie,' Marcel shouted.

'It is not a lie. He allowed me to take the ignition key from him, but as soon as I started the car he began to shoot at me. That is how I got this.' He touched the scar on his cheek.

'Even if what you say is true,' Valland said, 'I still don't understand why Marcel should do such a thing.'

'Because he's mad. He's a homicidal maniac. He likes to kill for the sake of killing. He murdered Toni, and that was good. But it was better still to make you believe that Georges Christophe was responsible for it, because then he could murder somebody else — on your orders. And you were so ready to believe.'

Marcel's mouth was open. He seemed to be trying to shout but there were no words coming out, only a thin trickle of saliva that dribbled down his chin.

'Look at his eyes,' Radford said. 'Can't you see he's mad? He killed Toni.'

Valland turned and smashed his clenched fist in Marcel's face.

'Dog!'

Marcel staggered against the door, and then with a movement so rapid it was like sleight of hand, he pulled out his pistol and shot Valland four times in the stomach. For a moment Valland stood where he was with a look of surprise on his face. Then his knees sagged and he slowly fell forward on to the carpet.

Marcel had his hand on the door-knob when Christophe shot him — calmly — like an executioner doing the necessary task. Then he turned to face Lamartine and raised the gun again.

'Do you intend to kill your own brother?' Lamartine said.

Christophe was taken aback by such an unexpected question. He stared at Lamartine in amazement. 'My God,' he said. 'So you admit it now. Now that you think it may help you.'

'I have never denied it,' Lamartine said.

Christophe held the gun balanced in his right hand. 'And so you think, because we both have the blood of that old sinner Pierre in our veins, that is good enough reason why I should spare your life?'

'I did not kill your wife and children.'

'You did not stop these swine from doing so.' He stabbed at the bodies with his foot. 'Do you deny that you urged them to do what they did?'

'I deny it,' Lamartine said.

'Of course. A man will deny anything to save his life.'

There was a knock on the door and the sound of a cough outside. Radford guessed that the servants had heard the shots and one of them had come to investigate. Lamartine glanced with a flicker of hope at the door. There was sweat on his forehead and Radford

249

knew that he was afraid.

The door-knob turned. The door opened an inch or two and was blocked by the bodies of Marcel and Valland. With a quick movement Christophe forced it shut again and turned the key in the lock.

'Now we will have no interruptions.'

'What good will it do you to shoot me?' Lamartine said.

'It is not a question of good. It is a question of justice.'

'Justice! You condemn me without trial. You execute me. What kind of justice is that?'

'What kind of justice is it to import an assassin to shoot a president?'

'He was an old man. He could not have lived much longer.'

'My children were not old.'

'I did not kill them.'

'You did not kill the President. But I shall kill you.' He lifted the automatic.

'No, Georges!' Radford said. He had pulled his hand out of his pocket and in his hand was the Smith and Wesson thirty-eight.

Christophe moved his gaze from Lamartine and looked at the revolver.

'So,' he said, 'you are on that side after all. In the end it is always white against coloured.'

'I am on no side,' Radford said. 'But there has been enough of killing.'

'Therefore, if I shoot him, you shoot me — to prevent further bloodshed? That is logic?'

'We are not discussing logic,' Radford said. But Christophe revealed the dilemma in which he found himself. There would be no point in shooting Christophe after Christophe had shot Lamartine. Christophe knew this, so in fact the revolver was no deterrent. It was a bluff, and Christophe had seen through the bluff. He turned his attention again to Lamartine, ignoring the revolver.

It was at this moment that Lebrun shouted a warning. 'Look!' He was pointing at the open window.

Radford swung round and saw Thomas framed in the opening, the light from the room falling on his thick, gorrilla-like body and the dark background of the night behind him. It was apparent now that Valland and Marcel had not dropped Thomas; they had merely left him outside, probably sitting in the car. No doubt he had heard the shooting and had crept warily round to the window, from which point he could view the situation before revealing himself.

There was a gun in Thomas's hand and he fired at the same moment as Lebrun yelled out his warning. The automatic dropped from

Christophe's hand and he clutched at his arm. Thomas fired again, and the bullet went past Christophe and smashed a picture on the wall behind him. Thomas did not have an opportunity to fire a third time because Radford shot him in the chest and he fell back into the darkness.

But Lamartine had been quick to seize his chance. He was still standing beside the heavy wooden chair which he had clutched when Christophe had struck him on the mouth. Now, with a quickness and strength that were perhaps a legacy of his younger and more athletic days, he lifted the chair with both hands, took three paces forward and brought it crashing down on Christophe's head.

Christophe fell to the floor and Lamartine seemed to go berserk, as though some killer instinct had got into him, or perhaps an urge to avenge the blow he had taken from his despised half-brother. Christophe's right arm had twisted under him at an unnatural angle, the bone possibly having been broken by Thomas's bullet. He tried to raise himself from the floor, but the chair smashed at him again.

Radford shouted at Lamartine: 'Stop it, Charles! You'll kill him.'

If Lamartine heard, he took no notice. He was breathing heavily and there was an expression of savagery on his face. He lifted the chair again.

Radford rushed at him, but there was another man who was quicker — Paul Lebrun.

To Lebrun Christophe was probably almost a god. He was the leader on whom rested all hope of a better standard of life. And here was this leader, this god, lying helpless on the floor and being battered to death by a white man, one of the hated capitalist class, the exploiters of Negro labour. For Lebrun there must have seemed only one course open. He had a knife in a leather sheath on his belt. He pulled out the knife and plunged it into Lamartine's back.

20

Pulling Out

Radford walked from the airport building and across the sunscorched concrete to the waiting air-liner. It was an American plane. There were a lot of Americans in evidence everywhere. For a time the airport had been out of action, with no aircraft arriving or departing. There had been a lot of bitter fighting on and around it, and some of the buildings showed the marks of grenades and small-arms fire. In the control tower there was hardly a sheet of glass left intact.

For a few days the struggle for power in St Marien had been brutal, bloody, and destructive. Then the Organization of American States, looking remarkably like the U.S. Marine Corps under another name, had stepped in to protect the lives and property of foreigners and to prevent communism from gaining another foothold in the Caribbean, and bloodshed and destruction had immediately become heavier.

But gradually the situation had been brought under control, and now the airport

254

and all the essential public services were working again, if not normally, at least with passable efficiency under the watchful eye of United States technicians and United States armed forces.

Throughout the world the communist press was still complaining angrily about yet another flagrant example of American imperialist aggression, but nobody was taking any military action to oppose it, and it was probable that nobody had ever had the slightest intention of doing so.

During the few days and nights of terror revolutionary mobs and army mutineers roamed the streets of Portneuf and other towns, fighting pitched battles with loyal troops and looting and setting fire to shops and private houses. General Madrin sent his meagre air force into action, but it was so difficult to distinguish friend from foe that as often as not they dropped their bombs or fired their machine-guns on the very men it had been their intention to assist.

In the country districts many estate owners banded together for protection, fortified their houses and fought off the attackers with rifles, shotguns and any other weapons that came to hand. Some of these fortified houses were set on fire and their occupants either burnt alive or cut to pieces with machetes as they tried to escape from the flames. The most bestial atrocities were reported as uncontrolled bands of men, drunk with temporary power and looted rum, roamed far and wide, turning one of the most beautiful areas of the world into an island of terror and carnage.

That Lamartine's house should have escaped was due largely to the fact that Christophe was there, recovering from his injuries. Moreover, now that Lamartine himself was dead, there was really little to excite the fury of the revolutionaries. The domestic employees remained at their posts, and after the first day or two things were really rather quiet in the big house even though occasional sounds of conflict could be heard in the distance.

The bodies of the dead men had been rather hastily buried, and Paul Lebrun, the Negro who had stabbed Lamartine, had disappeared and had not been seen again.

Radford himself had broken the news of her husband's death to Sophie Lamartine. A shiver had run through her body, but otherwise she had showed no emotion. She spoke calmly.

'I heard shooting. I suspected that something like this must have occurred. It was perhaps inevitable.' She turned her face towards him, and if he had not known that she was blind he would have supposed that she was staring at him. 'But you, Guy? You are not hurt?'

He assured her that he was not, and she gave a sigh of relief. 'Thank God! Oh, thank God for that!' She was silent for a moment or two; then she said: 'You must not think me callous if I do not weep for Charles. I hardly need to tell you that he has not been the best of husbands; and if he has now died by violence he has only himself to blame. He was a cruel man.'

'And yet you must have loved him once.'

'Loved him? How can I tell? I imagined so — at first. I was young then and knew so little of men. I had romantic dreams, as all young girls do; but it did not take long for those dreams to fade. I soon learned that he had married me only for the sake of the estate that I was to inherit from my father. For me he cared nothing.'

'I am sorry.'

'There is no need for you to be sorry.' She moved towards him and touched his face with her hand. 'What do you intend to do now? Will you leave St Marien?'

'I don't know. Perhaps it would have been better for everyone if I had never come.'

'You must not think that,' she answered

quickly. 'There are people here who will miss you greatly if you decide to go.'

He did not ask whether she were one of those who would miss him; he believed he knew the answer to that question.

'Also,' she said, 'we shall need a man capable of taking control.'

'I don't know that I am the right man.'

'I believe you are.'

'I will think it over,' he said.

★　★　★

Yvonne Christophe came to nurse her brother and was hospitably received by the two widows. Nicolette even remarked to Radford on the strange working of fate that had brought to the house another son and daughter of old Pierre to take the place of the ones who had been killed.

'The girl is lovely. I have never seen her before. I should hardly have believed it. And almost white. Quite remarkable.'

Christophe was in the room that had been Blond's. They had managed to get a doctor out from Portneuf to attend to him. The man had set Christophe's arm — the bullet had passed right through — and then had hurried back to the wounded who needed his services in the town.

'I doubt whether I shall be able to come again. There is so much to do and not nearly enough of us to do it.'

Christophe looked as though all the fire had gone out of him.

'I wish that the bullet had gone through my heart. I have nothing to live for.'

'You still have work to do,' Radford said.

'It is all ruined. This violence will achieve nothing. The whole island is in a state of chaos.'

★   ★   ★

Yet it was from this chaos that a man was thrown up — by what process of selection it was difficult to understand — and the man was Felix Porchaire. For some time Porchaire had been silent, apparently taking no hand in any of the momentous proceedings. Then, with the O.A.S. gradually restoring order, out of the obscurity in which he had been existing — where, no one seemed to know — Porchaire was pushed, was dragged, or stepped forward.

By the will of the people — President Porchaire!

They heard the announcement over the radio in the Lamartine library — Radford and the three women. Nicolette gave a laugh, half bitter, half amused. 'By the will of the people! What people? The Porchaire faction? Oh, he's a sly dog is Felix. Whatever happens, whoever goes under, Felix Porchaire swims to the top.'

'Do you think he will be able to hold the presidency?' Radford asked.

'Who is going to push him out? When this is over everyone will be too exhausted. They will be glad of someone to put the house in order.'

★ ★ ★

Later Porchaire himself spoke to the nation, and as he heard the deep voice booming out Radford remembered the man he had seen on only two occasions — so small, so dapper, with his curious mincing walk and his pale, soft hands.

'Citizens and countrymen of St Marien,' Porchaire said, 'as one who has taken no active part in the tragic affairs of the past week, as one who deplores the brutal and inexcusable assassination of President Petra and the terrible events that have succeeded it, I have come forward, greatly against my inclinations, but feeling in duty bound to answer the call of a suffering nation, to take over at this dark hour the onerous duties of the highest office in the land.'

It was a long opening sentence, but Porchaire managed it without difficulty. He even appeared to take pleasure in the rolling sonority of the phrases. They suited the pompous nature of the man, and to anyone who did not know the inner workings of this whole sordid business might even have sounded genuine. But to Radford, who had seen Porchaire coming away from the conference with Lamartine and Valland and Blond, the cynical falsity of the words was sickening.

'Now that order has been restored,' Porchaire went on, 'now that passions have had time to cool, I ask you, I beseech you all, to sink your differences and cease from wanton killing and destruction. Go back to work, pick up the scattered threads of our national life, make the wheels turn again and the mills grind. Go back, and I pledge you my word as an honourable gentleman that all your grievances will be heard with sympathy and understanding. Believe me, we who control the industry of St Marien are not monsters; it is our dearest wish that all should share in a prosperous and expanding economy. But this is not the way to prosperity. Not by bloodshed, not by riot, not by lawlessness, will our difficulties be solved.

Therefore I urge you to demonstrate to the world, whose eyes are now turned upon us, that we in St Marien are capable of ordering our affairs in the manner of civilized men and women.'

★ ★ ★

Radford went with Yvonne to tell Christophe the news. His reaction was similar to that of Nicolette.

'One might have known that little Porchaire would wriggle his way to the top.'

'He has promised to listen to the grievances of the people,' Yvonne said.

'Oh, he will listen. That will cost him nothing. But there will always be some reason why the time is not ripe for anything to be done.'

'Can Porchaire retain the presidency?' Radford asked. 'He can't have been constitutionally elected.'

'He will find some way of making his position secure.' Christophe sounded resigned.

'Then you will not fight him?'

'I have done with fighting.'

'But you are still secretary of the union.'

'I intend to resign.'

'No,' the girl said. 'You must not do that. You must not give up now. Think of all the men who look to you for leadership.'

Christophe was contemptuous. 'They are animals. Let them lead themselves. I have finished with them. If they want me to lead them, let them bring back my wife and children. I have sacrificed my family for them and I will do no more.'

Having said this, he turned and buried his face in the pillow. They went out of the room and left him to his despair.

Later the girl said: 'You will leave St Marien now. You will not come back.'

'I shall leave only if you leave with me,' Radford said.

'I cannot come with you.'

'Then I shall stay. I can have a job at the mine. Nicolette and Sophie have both urged me to stay.'

'It would be wiser to go.'

'Do you want me to go?'

'I don't want you to ruin your life.'

'Do you think it would ruin me to marry you?'

'I am half black,' she said, 'even though my skin is white.'

'I don't care about that. I love you.'

'You love me now. Later it may not be so. Later you may regret what you have done. I could not bear that.'

'I should never regret marrying you.'

'Suppose there were children. Suppose they were coloured.'

'There need be no children. You are all I need.'

'You have friends in England. Would you want them to know that your wife was the bastard daughter of a creole and a Negress?'

He winced to hear her speak like that. He said: 'No one would have to know.'

'Then you would be ashamed to tell them?'

'You're twisting my words,' he said. 'I should never be ashamed of you.'

'Think it over for three days. Think carefully over what I have said. If you decide to go away, I shall understand. It would be the wisest thing to do. And if you go, please don't say goodbye because that would be too hard to bear. Just go without a word.'

'I love you, Yvonne,' he said.

'And I love you. But love may not be enough.'

★   ★   ★

The concrete burned through the soles of his shoes. The great silver air-liner glittered in the sunlight. It made his eyes ache to look at it.

He had thought about it for three days. Yvonne had avoided him, leaving him to make his own decision. In the end he had seen that she was right. There were too many reasons why such a marriage would never work out. He loved her, but as she had said, love might not be enough. He had made his decision and had packed his bag.

He climbed up the steps and entered the air-liner. He had finished with St Marien and would never return. He sat down and tried to read a magazine, but the print was a blur. He closed his eyes, trying to shut out the world, to shut out everything.

'Ah, Monsieur Radford,' the voice said, wheezing a little. 'How pleasant, how very pleasant. And what a coincidence, no?'

He opened his eyes and looked up to see Monsieur Blond easing himself into the seat beside him. Blond was just as he had been when Radford had first seen him, just as plump, just as breathless, a shade pinker perhaps.

'I thought you were dead,' Radford said. He might have added that it would have given him great pleasure to have seen the earth being shovelled on to that pink, stout body. He personally would have helped to ram it down. But he did not say this.

Blond raised his pale eyebrows in faint surprise. 'Dead! Oh, no. Not at all. I have been resting for the past few days, while all this upheaval was taking place, you understand. Waiting for things to get back to normal. As normal as they can be in this kind of place.' He tittered delicately. 'Until now it was, of course, impossible to leave. The entire transport system was at a standstill.'

'And you wished to leave?'

Monsieur Blond gave a smile. 'But naturally. My business here is finished. In essentials it has been neither unsuccessful nor unprofitable — no, not at all unprofitable. Certain details — beyond my control, I may say — have been rather untidy; but — ' his plump shoulders rose and fell — 'it is of no importance.'

He drew a wheezy breath and laid one soft, pink hand on Radford's knee, where it lay like some malignant and faintly obscene growth.

'I see that you too are pulling out,' he said. 'Very wise, if I may say so, very wise. For a civilized man this is not really a suitable country. It is too violent, too angry. And the natives — truly little better than savages. Yes, you are very wise to have done with it.'

Radford pushed the hand from his knee. He got up.

'If you will excuse me,' he said.

Blond looked up in surprise. 'You are surely not thinking of leaving the plane. Not now. We are almost ready to start. If you get

266

out now you may be left behind.'

'That is just what I intend,' Radford said.

Outside the air-liner the sun hit him. He did not notice it. He began to walk across the concrete to the airport buildings. Someone shouted at him. It could have been Blond. He took no notice. He felt happier than he had been for the last three days.

THE END

Books by James Pattinson
Published by The House of Ulverscroft:

WILD JUSTICE
THE WHEEL OF FORTUNE
ACROSS THE NARROW SEAS
CONTACT MR. DELGADO
LADY FROM ARGENTINA
SOLDIER, SAIL NORTH
THE TELEPHONE MURDERS
SQUEAKY CLEAN
A WIND ON THE HEATH
ONE-WAY TICKET
AWAY WITH MURDER
LAST IN CONVOY
THE ANTWERP APPOINTMENT
THE HONEYMOON CAPER
STEEL
THE DEADLY SHORE
THE MURMANSK ASSIGNMENT
FLIGHT TO THE SEA
DEATH OF A GO-BETWEEN
DANGEROUS ENCHANTMENT
THE PETRONOV PLAN
THE SPOILERS
HOMECOMING
SOME JOB
BAVARIAN SUNSET
THE LIBERATORS
STRIDE

We do hope that you have enjoyed reading this large print book.

Did you know that all of our titles are available for purchase?

We publish a wide range of high quality large print books including:
Romances, Mysteries, Classics
General Fiction
Non Fiction and Westerns

Special interest titles available in large print are:
The Little Oxford Dictionary
Music Book
Song Book
Hymn Book
Service Book

Also available from us courtesy of Oxford University Press:
Young Readers' Dictionary
(large print edition)
Young Readers' Thesaurus
(large print edition)

For further information or a free brochure, please contact us at:
Ulverscroft Large Print Books Ltd.,
The Green, Bradgate Road, Anstey,
Leicester, LE7 7FU, England.
Tel: (00 44) 0116 236 4325
Fax: (00 44) 0116 234 0205

*Other titles in the
Ulverscroft Large Print Series:*

THE UNSETTLED ACCOUNT

Eugenia Huntingdon

As the wife of a Polish officer, Eugenia Huntingdon's life was filled with the luxuries of silks, perfumes and jewels. It was also filled with love and happiness. Nothing could have prepared her for the hardships of transportation across Soviet Russia — crammed into a cattle wagon with fifty or so other people in bitterly cold conditions — to the barren isolation of Kazakhstan. Many did not survive the journey; many did not live to see their homeland again. In this moving documentary, Eugenia Huntingdon recalls the harrowing years of her wartime exile.

FIREBALL

Bob Langley

Twenty-seven years ago: the rogue shoot-down of a Soviet spacecraft on a supersecret mission. Now: the SUCHKO 17 suddenly comes back to life three thousand feet beneath the Antarctic ice cap — with terrifying implications for the entire world. The discovery triggers a dark conspiracy that reaches from the depths of the sea to the edge of space — on a satellite with nuclear capabilities. One man and one woman must find the elusive mastermind of a plot with sinister roots in the American military elite, and bring the world back from the edge . . .

STANDING IN THE SHADOWS

Michelle Spring

Laura Principal is repelled but fascinated as she investigates the case of an eleven-year-old boy who has murdered his foster mother. It is not the sort of crime one would expect in Cambridge. The child, Daryll, has confessed to the brutal killing; now his elder brother wants to find out what has turned him into a ruthless killer. Laura confronts an investigation which is increasingly tainted with violence. And that's not all. Someone with an interest in the foster mother's murder is standing in the shadows, watching her every move . . .